Two-Step Devil

Two-Step Devil

A Novel

Jamie Quatro

Grove Press
New York

Wendell Berry, excerpt from, ["A young man leaving home"] from *This Day: Collected and New Sabbath Poems 1979-2012*. Copyright © 2004 by Wendell Berry. Reprinted with the permission of The Permissions Company, LLC on behalf of Counterpoint Press, counterpointpress.com. "Chattanooga Choo Choo," Music by Harry Warren, lyrics by Mack Gordon © 1941 (Renewed) Twentieth Century Music Corporation. All Rights Controlled by EMI Feist Catalog Inc. (Publishing) and Alfred Music Publishing Co., Inc. (Print). All Rights Reserved. Used by permission of Alfred Music. From the book *The Collected Poems: 1931–1987* by Czeslaw Milosz. Copyright © 1988 by Czeslaw Milosz Royalties, Inc. Used by permission of HarperCollins Publishers.

FIRST EDITION

Published simultaneously in Canada
Printed in the United States of America

The interior of this book designed by Norman E. Tuttle at Alpha Design & Composition.

This book was set in 12-pt. Sabon by Alpha Design & Composition of Pittsfield, NH.

First Grove Atlantic hardcover edition: September 2024

Library of Congress Cataloging-in-Publication data is available for this title.

ISBN 978-0-8021-6313-4
eISBN 978-0-8021-6314-1

Grove Press
an imprint of Grove Atlantic
154 West 14th Street
New York, NY 10011
Distributed by Publishers Group West
groveatlantic.com

24 25 26 27   10 9 8 7 6 5 4 3 2 1

For Ralph

Only a white-haired old man, who would be a prophet
Yet is not a prophet, for he's much too busy,
Repeats while he binds his tomatoes:
There will be no other end of the world,
There will be no other end of the world.

—Czesław Miłosz,
"A Song on the End of the World"

Prologue

Fetus in a Fist

1980–2014

The Prophet's wife had cramps. Late July, six weeks before the due date. They were coming on regular with twenty minutes between. The Prophet—his given name was Winston but he couldn't remember the last time anyone called him that—phoned Mae Thomas, who delivered babies free of charge and was said never to have lost a single infant soul. Mae Thomas asked if there was any bleeding or spotting, and when the Prophet said no, she told him it was either dehydration or Braxton-Hicks, likely both, and that his wife should drink orange juice, lie on her side, and practice deep breathing.

Two days later the Prophet's wife had a fever and couldn't make the baby move even after two Dr Peppers and hard pressing on the sides of her belly.

This time the Prophet walked the half mile to Mae Thomas's duplex in Hinkles. Mae drove him back out to his trailer, where his wife was curled on a mattress.

Mae Thomas listened with a stethoscope. She tugged on a glove and felt around inside.

The child's wrongway up, she said. You all need to get down to the hospital.

She handed him the keys to her truck. The Prophet was thirty-seven years old and, because of the drink, hadn't sat behind the wheel of a car in ten years. His wife did the driving when it was called for. But the Prophet found it was nothing to drive again, nothing at all, a kind of flying, natural, the tires barely touching asphalt all the way through Lookout Mountain and down Ochs Highway to Broad Street, on into the city to downtown until he saw the arrows pointing: HOSPITAL, EMERGENCY ENTRANCE, EMERGENCY DROP-OFF, EMERGENCY PARKING. His wife moaning beside him, taking in sharp sucks of air.

Sliding glass doors. They took his wife away.

The Prophet sat opposite a row of windows facing a propane plant on the other side of the river. Even from inside he could smell the sewage-like stench of the gas. A lavender dusk settled up around the bridges and behind the big houses on the hills, the air thick and gauzy with wet.

Two hours passed, and then a doctor and nurse came out. The nurse sat beside the Prophet and put a hand on his knee while the doctor explained that the fetus was long dead, the cord twisted up four times around its neck. He said it was much smaller than it should have been, had been festering inside his wife's uterus, and it was a good thing he'd brought her in before the infection spread. His wife was still asleep. They'd cleaned out her insides. The Prophet could go in and see her when she woke.

The doctor left. The nurse told him the baby was a girl with dark fuzz on her temples and a tiny extra thumb on her left hand. The Prophet decided not to tell his wife about the sex or temple fuzz or extra thumb unless she asked. She didn't ask. She sat in the wheelchair, mute and shivering, waiting for him to lift her into the truck.

The Prophet got his wife back up the mountain, carried her inside and laid her down on the couch. She looked to be asleep. He leaned over to put a folded pillow under her knees like the nurse told him, and as he stood the movie screen dropped in front of him, its bottom edge hovering an inch above his wife's body.

It was always the first thing he saw when the visions cut in on him: unscrolling fabric, clean-sheet white, five feet square.

On the screen was a planet Earth sketched in colored pencil, flat and messy, the way a child might draw it. Loose green shapes on a blue circle. Inside the Earth something was squirming around. A crack appeared at the equator, snaked down through the continent of Africa, and the planet split open like an egg. Knuckles, forearm, elbow: a fist and arm punching its way out. The fist came all the way down off the screen and rested on his sleeping wife's belly.

The hand opened. The Prophet looked.

The palm cradled a curled-up fetus, sticky with blood. A cord twisted out from its middle, metallic silver, like the pull chain on a lamp. The fetus gave off a high-pitched electric buzz. The skin was wax paper, seethrough, with blue-marbled veins like twisted-up vines inside. A faint light pulsed in its bald head. He saw the feeble quivering heart.

Spirit housed in meat! the Prophet heard his own voice say. Eternity sealed up in clay jars!

The hand closed, squeezing the fetus tight. The Prophet waited for it to pull back inside the Earth, but it punched into his wife's belly the same way it had punched itself out of the planet. His wife made a sound the Prophet recognized: an animal dying or in heat. *Out of rags, riches*—another voice, thousands of voices, the sound of a mighty waterfall—and then the hand was pulling back, the Earth was closing around the fist, the screen rolled up and disappeared and there was his wife with her eyes wide and all her teeth showing.

The Prophet saw his own hand was resting on her stomach.

Please take your hand off me, she said.

Four months later his wife still hadn't gotten her period. She went back to the doctor, who examined her, then drew blood to determine the due date.

Unusual, this soon after a D&C, but it happens, the doctor said.

The Prophet decided his drinking days were over. He bought himself a '75 Chevy G10 van in which to bring home his wife and baby. Zeke. A son, his only son, their child. Together they raised Zeke until his wife lost both breasts and her lymph nodes, shrank into a pained and weeping thing, and passed. Zeke was twelve. The Prophet felt he and his son should make a fresh start together, someplace untinged by memories of suffering. He sold the trailer and bought a parcel of densely forested land ten miles out the back of the mountain, across the Georgia border and into Alabama. A long driveway cut through the trees and opened on a sunlit clearing above a creek. Here there was a caved-in shack with a sagging front porch engulfed in kudzu. An oak trunk with its branches sawed off rose through the center of the ruin.

Looka there, the Prophet said to Zeke. We'll build us a cabin around the trunk like they done. Tree of life rising smack up through the middle of our house!

The cabin was one room, square, with a little kitchen annexed off the back. They used salvaged shipping crates for the walls, corrugated tin panels set over log beams for the roof. Once the cabin was finished and the windows put in—beveled glass, cast-offs they found at the junkyard—he and Zeke stripped the trunk of bark and sanded it to a silky gold sheen. They installed a wood-stove with a blower to circulate heat in the winter. In the kitchen they put in cupboards and counters and a stainless double sink, with a barrel to keep fresh water inside and another to collect rainwater outside. From yard sales and thrift stores they acquired furnishings: velour recliners and a little end table to set between them; folding lawn chairs for visitors and worn wooden rockers for the porch; twin mattresses, sheets, blankets, and pillows. Down the hill, toward the creek, they built a portable lean-to and hauled down a porcelain toilet with a cracked tank to set over the hole.

When everything was finished, the Prophet prayed. Now my hard times is done with, Lord, he said. You gave me a painful cross to bear when I could stand up under it. But now, as I'm old, in your mercy you suffered to remove it. Myself and the son what you've given me, the both of us growing old into glory, your servants unto death.

In the summers they grew vegetables and sold them to tourists who drove up Lookout Mountain to see Rock City and Ruby Falls. TURN HERE 4 TOMATOS. In the afternoons and evenings, the Prophet and his son sat on the front porch and played guitar and sang hymns, Zeke with a throat full of wonders, a voice that made tourists pay three times what they should for the baskets of vegetables they carried off. At night they worked on painting his visions. So far he'd hung the vision of the fist punching through the cracked Earth, and his very first vision, an unfinished bridge with people falling off. He hung the cupboard Zeke had painted before his mama passed: a shark with its mouth open, gobbling up falling stars.

Ten years went by in peace. And then Johnny Cash died, so instead of hymns Zeke began to sing Cash, song after song, his voice sounding exactly like the Man in Black himself. Tourists shot videos and put them on the internet system and his son's voice reached the bigwigs in Nashville. The bigwigs drove out to the cabin and took Zeke for a ride in a Denali with a TV in the back, showing him the many stages of the world he might like to perform on, dressed like Cash reincarnated.

Zeke was twenty-two. He moved to Nashville and sang Johnny Cash on stages around the city. He got married and had a little girl named Sullivan. The Prophet went to see her when she was born: a swipe of dark hair at one end of a rolled-up blanket, squinched-shut eyes and a little red bite on the forehead. It was the only time he ever saw her.

Now it was 2014. Zeke thirty-three, Sullivan almost eight. The Prophet put hard candy into envelopes and mailed them to her whenever he could. Sometimes he put in a dollar bill. Seventy years the planet had spun him around only to set him down here, alone in the back-woods of Alabama, sending out the one-way envelopes.

In the daytime he kept busy with his vegetables and painting, but at night the loneliness for Zeke and his long-gone wife—even loneliness for the woman in the brothel he visited, back when he was a regular devil like the rest—sometimes that loneliness would creep inside the cabin. Dark smoke seeping between cracks in the wall planks, clouds of it fogging up the place and blurring his paintings. When this happened he'd get out his guitar and sing hymns to make the smoke pull back. Sometimes it worked. Other times the smoke hardened into the dark shape of Two-Step Devil crouched in the corner beside the woodstove.

Look at you, Two-Step would begin. *Third-grade educated, a-fooling yourself with all this vision talk.*

Look at you, spending your last years alone with a brain wasted on drink.

Get behind me, you old-time accuser, the Prophet would say. But once Two-Step had taken up his place in the corner, it was impossible to get him to leave. And so the Prophet would lay down his guitar, crawl onto his mattress, and wrap a pillow around his ears until Two-Step gave up or the Prophet fell asleep. Whichever thing happened first.

Prophecy

Look at the stars! look, look up at the skies!
O look at all the fire-folk sitting in the air!
The bright boroughs, the circle-citadels there!

—Gerard Manley Hopkins, "The Starlight Night"

He Builds His Ezekiel Machine

2014

The Prophet stood on his porch, taking in the landscape. The soft earth was shooting up green everywhere he looked. Purple blossoms furred the redbuds along his driveway; here and there beneath them were sprays of yellow forsythia. Soon the cherries would be out. At the far edge of his field a high-up breeze swayed the tips of the Georgia pines. Above them, the sky was cloudless, with a pale three-quarter moon like a shell beneath water. A fine afternoon! He would drive down to the junkyard to look for the saw blade he needed to finish his Ezekiel machine.

The machine was a working model of the spinning wheels he'd been carrying around inside his head as long as he could remember. They were glow-in-the-dark green and overlapped like the Olympic symbol, but instead of five there were twelve. Whenever he closed his eyes he could see them there, spiraling like gears at the center of his forehead. For a long time he didn't know what they meant. But after Zeke left, the Prophet got back to reading the Bible. He skipped most of the books in the front and only skimmed the Psalms and Proverbs. But the big-time prophets got him excited. Here was God sitting above the circle of the Earth with people hopping around beneath him like grasshoppers; here were men looking at each other with their faces on fire, Jerusalem a woman in dirty skirts! In Ezekiel he read about the interlocking wheels with rims of eyeballs, and how the wheels followed after four creatures—man, lion, ox, and eagle. How it was the *spirits* of those creatures that made the wheels move. What he'd been seeing all these years was the Holy Spirit. The way the wheels behaved was a kind of checks-and-balances system by which he could tell if the Spirit was pleased. If the wheels were bright and moving toward him, it meant a vision would be coming on soon and he was God's chosen instrument to receive it. If he saw only a smear of light, or, worst of all, darkness, he would lie on his belly and beg. Lord, Lord, he'd say. Don't leave me to myself. Don't do me like Saul and depart.

In this way he learned how hard you had to work to keep the Spirit happy.

He got in his van and drove out to the highway, crossing the border from Alabama into Georgia and taking Nickajack Road to the base of the mountain. It was warmer down here, the dogwoods with their little white plates already laid out on branches. At the junkyard in Flintstone he pulled through the open gate and parked beside the abandoned office. There was the truck door he'd found last time, propped where he'd left it. The door had a picture of a bucket dumping red paint onto the globe, with COVER THE EARTH stenciled in white letters. He wished he felt good enough to lift it into his van.

He walked along the chain-link fence separating the junkyard from an access road. The fence was eight feet high, with plastic straps woven through and magnolia trees planted along its length—fence and trees meant to hide the junkyard from a tract home development across the road. The development had failed. They'd cleared the field and stubbed out a few homes before the market crash. Now, six years later, the field was all weeds and skeletal rebar sticking up from dirty concrete.

A circular blade the size of a plate you might set under a teacup. That's what he was looking for. Teeth with a good thick kerf, nothing too rusted. He had eleven blades with spindles through their centers laid out and ready. When he found the twelfth—the smallest, which he thought of as his Benjamin blade—he'd attach a battery-powered motor to make it spin. The teeth on the smallest blade would intersect with those on the next, bigger in size. And that blade would spin the one beside it. And so on. Small as a mustard seed but able to move mighty equipment! He liked the idea of using thrown-away saw blades to make his machine.

Instruments of destruction reclaimed for a holy purpose. Something fallen raised up higher than it was before.

He walked up and down along the fence, toeing up scrap metal here and there. He didn't feel much like bending over. His left side was hurting him bad today. When he drew a breath his chest made an *oooooh* sound.

The sun was just starting to lower over the mountain when he heard tires on gravel. Through an opening in the fence where two straps had rotted out, he saw a black Mercedes pull up to the abandoned gas station on the other side of the access road. It parked between the convenience store and a shed with the word FEED spray-painted on its side. The passenger door opened and a thickset man with a short beard and mustache got out. He wore a buttoned vest over a long-sleeve shirt, khaki shorts, and white athletic sneakers with tube socks to his knees. The socks had red stripes at their tops, two slashes across each shin.

The woman who got out of the driver's side had short spiky hair dyed the color of a Coca-Cola can. She wore a white T-shirt and cutoff jean shorts and flip-flops. She was younger than the man—thirty, maybe—with a big bust and tire fat in her stomach. She plucked at her shirt and dragged on her cigarette; the Prophet caught a whiff of the smoke and it mixed with the stench of trash and metal and the sickly sweet scent of the magnolia blossoms, still white at the treetops but browning near the ground. Dead leaves like charred bits of paper crackled around his ankles. He stood still so as not to make any noise.

He'd better watch these people awhile.

The man went around behind the store, where the old bathroom was. The Prophet had used that bathroom himself. The stall door was broken and there was no running water but the urinal drained fine. The store had been boarded up around the same time the development failed. A few faded stickers still clung to the windows: WE ACCEPT FOOD STAMP BENEFITS. UNDER 18 NO TOBACCO. WE CARD. Above the gas pump was a red-and-white bird, its neck and wings stretched out like it was soaring over the station. PURE FIREBIRD YOUR PURCHASE 00.00 GALLONS 00.00. Forsaken like the rest of the town, with its for-sale Baptist church and empty dog hotel, its fenced run grown thick with pokeweed. Tilly's Acres. He'd never met Tilly but he remembered the dogs.

The woman stood there, dragging on her cigarette. The man returned and got a can of beer out of the front seat. He walked over to the church with its peeling white paint and empty parking spot marked RESERVED FOR PASTOR & WIFE, raised his can like he was making a toast, then tipped it so a swallow of beer poured out and bubbled on the dirt.

The woman dropped her cigarette and opened the rear door. The Prophet saw long legs and bare feet. The girl who stepped out looked like a teenager. She was taller than both the woman and the man, thin, with messy dark hair falling around her face and shoulders, reaching almost to her elbows. She wore a long yellow sundress with spaghetti straps that fell down around her arms. She pushed them up, but they fell again.

Kingston, the woman said. Where'd you put them pills?

The man reached into his vest pocket and tossed something that rattled. The woman caught it, took the girl by the elbow, and walked her around behind the store.

Only time the Prophet ever saw any kind of traffic on the access road was in fall, when the corn maze and haunted forest opened to tourists. He could walk down along the fence to the open gate, then across the access road and back to the gas station. People call me the Watchman, he'd say. Who might you be?

The Prophet waited, and when they came back he saw the girl had changed into a short dress that sparkled like flashbulbs when she moved. She wore high-heeled sandals with straps around the ankles and had her hair piled up on top of her head. The woman and girl got into the back seat together; the man got behind the wheel. When they pulled onto the access road the Prophet caught a glimpse of the girl's face in the rear window. She had her hands up like she was about to sneeze or push her hair behind her ears.

There were zip ties on her wrists.

The car headed out toward Chattanooga. No license plate.

The Prophet's heart stuttered against his rib cage. He tried to take shallow breaths but the coughing overtook him. His eyes watered and he tasted metal. With his back against the fence he sat in the crackling magnolia leaves and waited for the fit to be over.

Only a glimpse. But he knew who the girl was: an angel of God. One of His Innocents. He knew what she needed was rescue from the man in the vest and the woman with the Coca-Cola hair.

He knew he was the one supposed to rescue her.

Here you've given me a real-life vision, Lord, the Prophet said aloud. You called me to be a major prophet, waiting for the Big Fish to come. But now I see you're calling me to be a minor prophet in the meantime. A Hosea to rescue the whore Gomer. Who wasn't a whore in your eyes.

Back When Two-Step Devil Showed Up

2000

The Prophet chewed his food on the side where he had four teeth on bottom and two on top. The other side was just gums and a loose flap of skin dangling from his top lip—a drained abscess left over from when a yellow jacket flew between his lips and stung him on the roof of his mouth. The infection had filled his gums and eaten out the roots of his top teeth. He forgot about the skin flap until someone looked at it funny. Then he'd tell how it happened. The flap stuck to his bottom lip if he didn't remember to wet it with his tongue before he spoke.

He sketched his visions in pencil on whatever he could find: cardboard boxes, newspaper, scraps of plywood. When he got a sketch the way he liked, he painted over it. Recently he'd finished three small paintings on white paper, all showing a donkey with wings standing on planet Earth. Celebrating Donkey, Big-Tears Donkey, Bags-of-Trouble Donkey. He'd grown fond of the animal, the way he kept showing up. Painting him was like spending time with a friend.

Visitors came for the fruits and vegetables he laid out on his front porch rails and upturned barrels. Watermelons and onions and potatoes in the late summers; in the fall, pumpkins and squash and knobby marbled-colored gourds. He'd got his first set of seeds from Doug and Pam Wilkins at Sun and Shade. Doug and Pam were Pentecostals. The Prophet didn't trust any religious organization. Most kinds of churches didn't understand his way of seeing, but at least the Pentecostals believed his visions were from the Lord.

His tomatoes were bestsellers. He grew them in baskets hanging from hooks twisted into the beams above his porch. He'd pulled off the tin roofing in places so sunlight and rain could get through. The dangling tomatoes ripened free of spots and the puckers that came from lying on the dirt or pressing against cage wire. The Lookout Mountain folks—rich, outdoorsy types, mostly Presbyterian—liked their tomatoes pristine. They liked to think it was something special to drive twenty-five miles out the back of the mountain, through Tennessee and Georgia and on into Alabama to buy tomatoes from a prophet who'd fill a basket and, for no extra charge, show them something of God's intentions for the planet's final days.

The Prophet would sit in his porch rocker and wait for customers. If he thought he heard tires, he'd stand.

Often he'd forget about the dangling plants and a tomato
would knock him on the head, and when this happened
his first thought was that God or a perturbed angel was
rapping him to remind him to stop sinning in his thought
life. His sins were mostly those of the mind, the evils
he'd like to do. Sins of commission. He hadn't had much
opportunity for commission in near a decade. It was the
sin-memories that snuck up on him; that was what he had
to confess, why God/angel/tomato had to get his attention. The thought of a prostitute's warm breast—a woman
he used to spend his paychecks on at the old brothel in
Chattanooga—that image would trigger a surge down
in his crotch and he'd have to put out a hand to steady
himself, or lean over his shovel. Hoo-whee, Lord, the
Prophet would say when he felt the tap on his head. Then
he'd fix his thoughts on his dead wife's breasts before the
doctors took them off and speak to whichever tomato had
knocked him: Even you are an instrument of the Lord.
God weren't ashamed to be a baby in a trough, and he
ain't ashamed to use a vegetable as his messenger.

Now it was August, morning, the sun just above the
trees. They were full up with tomatoes this year, enough
to sell three or four dozen every day and jar the rest for
winter. He had a nice set of onions he'd just harvested,
plus seven long watermelons he'd brought in yesterday.

The Prophet stepped into his pants and slippers and
pulled on a white undershirt. He got a can of warm
Coke from the case beside his mattress and went out to

the porch. Too early to expect any visitors, but at least out here he might catch a breeze. He sat in his rocker and leaned over to set the can down. The movie screen dropped in front of him, same as always when a vision cut in. Clean-sheet white, five feet square.

A black-and-white film began: two rectangles rising from a slab of concrete. At the top of each rectangle grew a spike like a toothpick. Standing atop one of the rectangles was a thin figure wearing boots and a bolo tie. His cowboy hat was pulled low, shading his face.

Line-drawn clouds drifted onto the screen from one side and off again at the other. The cowboy stood there, motionless. A cloud snaked a circle around his bent head before swimming off again. The cowboy removed his hat and held it against his chest, then made a low bow like he was up on some stage, hearing applause. The Prophet could see the top of his skinny bald head. The cowboy replaced the hat and began to dance, a country two-step, thumbs hooked into his belt loops. His heels click-clacked together on the edge of what the Prophet realized was a skyscraper.

I'm a-goin' after the people, the dancing cowboy sang in time with his jigging feet.

I'm, a-goin', after, the people.

I do believe you are dancing on the Tower of Babel, the Prophet said.

A bird—an enormous goose—appeared at the corner of the screen. It was stuffed like a Thanksgiving turkey, its wings wired together across its back. A second goose came in behind it, stuffed and wired the same way, flying lower than the first.

The geese picked up speed, keeling right, left.

The cowboy stopped his two-stepping.

You seeing what I'm a-seeing? he asked the Prophet.

The Prophet felt his own voice vibrate in his throat: What do you think you're doing, you two-stepping devil?

Your name, the cowboy said, *is top of the list of them what's to be done away with!* The cowboy jumped off the movie screen; the geese jammed themselves into the rectangles, one bird tail sticking out the side of each; the screen lurched forward and covered the Prophet like a blanket, smothering him. He smelled smoke and saw nothing but white, then gray, gray, gray.

His chest burned. He couldn't draw a breath. Left side, left side, something was chewing him up in there!

He tore at the blanket and found himself sitting in the rocker, spilled Coca-Cola in a puddle beside him. He gulped some air.

This is something bad's gonna happen, he said aloud. I got to get this one down in paint.

Rescue I

2014

The Prophet drove to the junkyard in Flintstone every afternoon for the rest of the week. He made a show of rooting around in piles but never strayed too far from the spot he'd first seen the Mercedes. Once he heard tires on gravel and ran to the rotted-out opening, but it was only a minivan with Florida plates. The rear door slid open and a shirtless boy got out. He took a piss on the privet beside the shed with the FEED sign and scrambled back into the car, the door sealing him away.

With each day the girl didn't show up, he began to think maybe he wasn't called to rescue, like Hosea. Well, that was okay. He was still a big-time prophet like Ezekiel and Daniel. The Big Fish was still coming.

When he returned from the junkyard he tried to finish his latest board, a sheep with its mouth hooked and held open by God's right hand. The other hand— God's left—was stuffing a lamb inside the sheep's mouth.

Across the top, in pencil, he'd written FEED MY SHEEP.
Now he was going over the letters in black paint. He kept
setting down the paintbrush to move the oil lamp so he
could see the pencil marks. He knew the interpretation:
the world needed to feast on the Lamb, Jesus Christ.
God had to pry open the world's mouth or they'd never
eat. But tonight, the more he looked at the painting, the
more the lamb looked like the girl. He sketched a long
skirt on the sheep, and some hair down the sides of its
face. Yes, the lamb was the girl, the sheep the men who
bought her—and the hand shoving her in was the man
in the vest and tube socks!

He dropped the paintbrush into the jar of water
with the other brushes and lay on his mattress, thinking of the girl's bare legs and dangling sundress straps
and long hair on either side of her face, like the temple
curtain rent in two—the holy of holies shining out of
her eyes, God's presence visible between lengths of torn
fabric. It was no use working on a hooked-mouth sheep
when in his head was the girl and her useless sundress
straps and temple-of-God hair.

Beside his bed the Prophet kept a notebook, lined
pages with wire rings. He turned to a fresh page and tried
sketching a few heads. He made some oval, like fat potatoes, and some like radishes, hearts with divots in their
tops. Neither shape was right. He tried circles, squares,
triangles. He tried adding eyes and ears and mouths. It
was hopeless. He didn't know the first thing about how

to draw a face. He could hardly manage to figure which side the thumb went on when he drew a hand.

He rolled off the mattress and got up on his knees.

Lord, you mark every sparrow, he said. I ask you to let me rescue this one fallen sparrow out of thousands. One of your innocents, a chaste virgin no matter how many times she's been violated. Let me be your thief, let me capture her, not for greed or any tainted purpose. To care for her as a father cares for his children.

I will speak tenderly to her in the desert, he prayed. Only show me when to go forth.

The next afternoon he drove to the junkyard and parked beside the office as usual. Tuesday, exactly a week since he'd seen the girl. An overnight rain had left the day hot and muggy. Mosquitoes buzzed his ears. He swiped at them and looked up at the back side of the Fairyland Club, where Zeke used to work: tables on the dining patio, twinkle lights strung overtop, citronella torches along the rail. He'd stopped hunting for the smallest saw blade. Working on the Ezekiel machine seemed unimportant now. Maybe he wasn't meant to finish. Maybe the machine was God's way of getting him to the right place at the right time. He thought of the worker in the Bible who buried the one talent he was given and was cast into outer darkness. He didn't want to be like that man. He'd always felt sorry for him. The worker given five talents and the worker given two had it easy: someone hands you a lot of something, you can stand to take some risks with it. But someone hands you one thing to take care of, just one small thing: Wasn't it better to protect it? Apparently that wasn't God's way. Well done, good and faithful servant—that's what the man with five and the man with two heard. What he wanted to hear.

He should finish what he'd started.

Using a length of PVC pipe, he began to prod around in piles. He wandered away from the fence, moving things here and there, trying to trick himself into caring about the smallest blade—it was like a performance he was making for himself, or maybe for God—and when he heard the tires, in his hurry to get back to the fence he tripped and fell over an upturned fender. He scrambled up and ran to the opening, ignoring the sting in his hands and knees.

It was there, the Mercedes, if he'd gone off any farther he might've missed it!

The man was standing in the pastor's parking spot, his back to the junkyard. When he turned around the Prophet saw he'd shaved off the beard but still had the mustache. He was wearing a dark suit—wool, maybe. The woman stood beside the car, smoking a cigarette like before. Her spiky hair was hidden beneath a shiny black wig but he could tell it was the same woman by her height and build.

All right, Lord, the Prophet whispered. All right.

He had a small mirror, the kind women used to powder their noses. He'd been careful to slide it into his pocket each day. He'd also painted the word RESKU on a cut piece of plywood and left it near the opening in the fence, inside an old car tire. He'd made sure the word fit in the open space where the fence straps were missing. He hoped he'd made the letters big enough for her to see. He hoped the girl knew how to read.

He peered at the car. Dimly, through the tinted back window, he saw a head with curly light hair. His heart double-timed. A different girl? Or maybe a wig, like the Coca-Cola woman's? She was still sucking her cigarette. Her back was to him. Now was his chance.

He held the mirror so that it caught the lowering sun.

One, two, three flashes onto the back seat window.

The woman stubbed out her cigarette and opened the door. Again the Prophet saw the long legs and sandals with hectic strings tied loose about the ankles. The same sparkly dress. It had to be her. The girl was facing his direction, rubbing her eyes, and then—glory—she yanked off the blond curls to reveal the temple-of-God hair piled on top of her head.

The Prophet flashed quickly on the ground in front of her feet.

One, two, three.

The girl looked toward the fence. For the first time the Prophet saw her face straight on: clear skin and bones high up in her cheeks, a small off-center nose, and wide-set eyes that drooped a little at their corners. She didn't look anything like he'd imagined. But she was pretty.

Not beautiful, not yet, but someday when she was an adult, that's the word he might choose.

The woman turned away, blowing smoke.

All right.

He put his face in the fence opening and smiled. He wanted the girl to know his smile meant: I am your friend and you can trust me. He held up the sign so it filled the opening. RESKU. He couldn't tell if she saw. She stood there motionless, and when the woman flicked away her cigarette and took the girl by the elbow to walk her around back, she only bowed her head.

The man was punching on a cellular. Had to be baking himself inside that suit. Five minutes passed, ten. The woman and the girl came back around the shed. Now the girl was barefoot and walking on her tiptoes, holding her strappy high heels in one hand. She had the blond wig back on, with a metal clip that sparkled like her dress. Her mouth was painted red.

She was looking in his direction.

He held up the sign.

RESKU.

The girl threw her head back and laughed. The sound was deeper than he thought a girl could make, like a croupy cough, *howhowhow*. The woman pushed her toward the car while she kept making the sound, *howhow-howhowhow*; the man walked over and put his face up to hers—even with her shoes off the girl was taller—and said something into her ear. She made the sound again. The man took a step backward, lurched forward, and pushed his fist into her stomach. The girl fell to sitting on the ground, like someone had shoved a chair into her knees from behind. She rolled to her side and lay still.

Lot of low things he'd seen but never a grown man punch a child. For a second he thought he would shout and climb over the fence. But he wasn't strong enough to climb, and if he shouted they'd be onto him; they'd get in the car and drive away and stop bringing the girl here. He took a breath in, feeling the sharp jab up beneath his ribs. The girl was feeling pain, too. In this way they were connected.

The woman was helping the girl up, folding her back into the car. The man got behind the wheel.

The Prophet flashed desperately at the back seat window.

One, two, three.

Looka here, he whispered. Looka here.

The girl's hand lifted—with a finger she touched the window—and then her face was pressed to the glass. Beneath the dark smears of her eyes her mouth was shaping words. He could hear the words inside his head, like listening to his own thoughts, and long after the car had backed up and spun its tires and turned onto the road toward Chattanooga, he could hear the words still repeating: *Help me, help me.*

A lit coal sat on his head. The heat poured into his ears and spilled down his cheeks, a liquid fire finding its way into the crack between his lips and burning his tongue. He licked his abscess flap and sucked in some air.

It wasn't two separate callings the Lord had given him, one to wait for the Big Fish, and one to rescue the girl. He was a major prophet like Ezekiel with his visions, and he was a minor prophet like Hosea rescuing Gomer, and they were the same calling, because the girl—he knew it, he knew it, how had he not realized?—the girl *was* the Big Fish he'd been waiting for.

Glorious! God was always starting with twos and turning them to one. Male and female one flesh. Jew and Gentile one nation. Heaven and Earth one city—the New Jerusalem.

He'd cast out the line. She'd reached for it. Touched it with a finger. That connection sent the words from the girl's mouth directly to his head. How to get the line back out to her? How to get her to grab on so he could reel her in? That's what he had to figure out.

Well, now he knew some things. He knew it was Tuesdays they drove through Flintstone. He knew they got her ready in the bathroom behind the gas station. He knew their routine, they didn't know he knew, and if he could somehow get her away and take her up the back roads to his cabin, he'd take care of her for a while. Treat her tenderly as his own grandchild. He would show her his boards and explain what was coming at the End, so that even after he was gone, the meaning of the prophecies would be safe inside her head.

It was growing dark. He drove up the mountain, reminding himself not to speed. He had to pull over twice to cough and wipe his mouth.

Slow down, old man, he said aloud. You got a whole week.

Inside the cabin he filled his lamp and lit the wick. He meant to make out his plan right away but he could only pace back and forth, clearing his throat. He couldn't remember the last time his nerves had him strummed up like this. He'd never be able to sleep. He'd stay awake all night if he had to, he would get calm and think things through. He'd make a list.

He put a hand on the smooth tree of life to steady himself. He'd always meant to paint the trunk with flowering vines. A few weeks ago he'd started sketching some on the ceiling above the trunk. Now he imagined the room full of color: vision boards on the walls, the ceiling covered with twisting plants. What a thing it would be, for the girl to open her eyes each morning and see nothing but leaves and branches and flowers.

In one corner, where the wall met the ceiling, he'd painted a stick figure of himself holding a fishing pole and a watering can. In the other corner, across the room diagonally, he'd painted the Big Fish. The Big Fish vision had come five years ago. He'd been planning to string some actual fishing line between the two corners, with a real-life hook nailed up into the fish's painted mouth.

But that idea wasn't quite right.

He got a pencil and dragged the stepladder over to Big Fish corner. He climbed up and, using a light stroke, sketched shoes on the fish's underbelly, two in front and two in back. He drew them plain and boxy, like square-toed boots. BIG FISH WALKING, he wrote beneath.

All this time he'd been waiting for the hook to land. But it was never going to get there by itself. Big Fish had to take steps. He climbed down and got a small brush and some paint, then went over the shoes and the words in black, and when he finished he lay on his mattress and pulled his blanket up to his chin and looked up at the shoes and the words. He felt pleased with himself in a new, shy way. No movie screen. The shoes were something he'd thought up himself.

His T-shirt was soaked through with sweat but he couldn't tell if he was hot or cold. He clutched the blanket up around his neck. So. The girl would take steps. She would grab the line and start walking toward him and he would reel her the rest of the way. And when he got her here he would show her the fish painting. This is you, he'd say. And that over there is me.

The girl would see with the eyes of her heart. She would understand the urgency and take the visions, the important ones, to the president with the face he trusted.

A young girl come all that way to speak to him! He would get on the radio and television and punch up his internet system and send out a message: Wake up, America. Get out of bed and listen.

From the darkness in the corner came a chuckle.

First drawing you made with any truth to it. A fish with feet. You're preaching evolution without even knowing.

The Prophet rolled to his side and pulled the blanket up over his ear.

See what happens when you trust what's inside your own head!

Vision of the Big Fish

2009

The Prophet was putting in main crop potatoes. Pam Wilkins at Sun and Shade gave him two crates full of russets, already chitted. In exchange he gave her a colored-marker drawing of a woman climbing a ladder set against a cherry tree, with twelve empty baskets on the grass around her. She's gonna fill up them baskets, the Prophet told Pam, and give away the fruit. We got to climb into the high reaches of the gospel, see, he said. We got to pluck from it and take the fruit into the world.

Pam put the picture inside a chalkboard frame. She wrote SPREAD THE FRUIT in white chalk and hung it in front of the cash register, where it covered the NO CHECKS EXCEPTED, NO EXCEPTIONS sign.

The sun was out, the morning air crisp. He'd already dug the trench. Pockets of mist hovered above the turned dirt like tiny exhales. The seed potatoes with their pocked eyes and gray-black chits sat in egg cartons on the uneven soil beside him. One by one he began to set the potatoes into the ground, giving each a command: Go forth and multiply. When it turned hot and the tater bugs started crawling up the leaves, he'd ask Samantha Simms to come pluck them off. She picked for him every year, bringing along her father, Render Simms, who was diabetic and blind and navigated the world holding on to a bamboo pole like a man at the prow of a riverboat. Samantha would get her father settled into a rocker and go pinch bugs while the Prophet sang Render the healing song. "I Heard the Sound of A-Goin' in the Mulberry Tree." He made up the verses as he went: The Lord our God is present, he is mighty to save. Jesus Christ is coming, he will set you free. Every so often he liked to mix in some Johnny Cash: Father hen is coming to call his chickens home. One hundred million angels come for you and me.

You're gonna sing the spirit of blindness right out of me! Render would say. But it was twelve years gone now and Render was blind as the first day he came. Had the shakes, too. You got to be patient with the sickness, the Prophet told him and Samantha. Thousand years is like a day, a day like a thousand years. Time, times, and half a time. God's seasons are not ours to understand.

The Prophet finished with the first set of potatoes and began to shovel the loose dirt overtop. Each eye on a potato would yield several plants. And those potatoes, in turn, would yield others. Potatoes were like generations of people. The gospel spread this way too. You told one

person, and that person told two others, and those two
told four. And so on. A single potato could throw a net
out big enough to cover the world.

He filled a bucket and began watering, walking
along the raised scar of dirt. One of these days he'd lay
in some irrigation hoses. When he reached the end of the
trench he looked up. At the far edge of his field, where
the walnuts and pine trees began, an ocean wave lifted
itself from the dirt.

Guess you done away with the movie screen, Lord,
he said.

The wave rose ten, twenty feet, frothing at the tip
but showing no signs of breaking. Higher it rose, until
the tallest pines were hidden behind the foamy crest.
The wave stood there, gathering itself in a mighty heap.

Here I am, the Prophet finally said.

From inside the wave came a voice: *What is in your
hand?*

He looked down and saw that he was holding a
fishing rod with a reel the size of a car tire. Dangling
from the hook was a tater bug.

That's something new, the Prophet said, a tater bug
for bait!

Cast and reel, the voice said.

Inside the wall of water were thousands of fish,
flickering and flashing like glitter. The Prophet cast and
set the line. Immediately he felt a hit. The fish he reeled
in was a minnow the size of his thumb. He dropped it

beside the leftover seed potatoes. He fished until the wave was empty and thousands of minnows lay at his feet. From the sparkling quivering pile came wet sucking sounds. But all together the fish amounted in size to no more than a large catfish.

Cast and reel.

Wave's empty, Lord—but as he said the words he saw that the churning wave held an enormous shape. Long as his field and tall as his cabin.

I'm gonna need a stronger line, the Prophet said.

My grace is sufficient! The voice shook the ground. The Prophet snatched up one of the little fish, threaded the hook through its eye socket, and cast. The bait soared up against the blue sky, twisting in the sunlight, shards of reflected light crackling over the field. The spool emptied and still the bait dangled in midair.

This here big fish is too far away, he said.

Is my arm too short? The voice was a two-by-four knocking him solid across the head; the pain sent him onto his back so that he lost hold of the pole. The wave towered over him, a blue dome with the sun glowing white behind, and then it broke and he was beneath the ocean. He couldn't swim. He tasted salt and felt pressure build in his ears and throat and lungs. Which way was up? He kicked toward where he'd last seen the sun; his foot hit something solid, a wall, a rock—

But he'd only kicked over the bucket of water. The field was as he'd left it.

Not watching a movie, but being part of it—this was urgent! He ran to the cabin. Where were his pencils? He had to get this one down. The vegetables and the singing, the visitors it had brought him so far: small fish. But a big fish was coming. Someone high up and powerful. Big Fish would see how the Prophet had already predicted things. Big Fish would tell the new president about things yet to come, the visions of the Earth's last days. This president would listen. He'd seen the man's picture in a newspaper, one hand lifted, the other on a red Bible. The new president had a face he could trust. The only face he could trust in all of Washington.

He ripped off the side of an old cardboard box and began to sketch the fish inside the wave, imagining himself as an observer above, looking down. The fish came out with a rectangular head and a tail shaped like a bow tie. He'd fix it later. He drew himself as a stick figure, holding a long pole with a fat reel.

When he finished, he stepped back to look at what he'd drawn. Only then did he smell the smoke.

I don't even need to tell you how ridiculous you are. Two-Step was in his corner beside the woodstove, hat pulled low over his face.

The Prophet turned back to his drawing. He lifted his pencil and—exaggerating the movement so Two-Step would see—drew a dark line coming out from his pole. He made the line arc up, half a rainbow, stopping in the middle space between himself and the fish. He traced over and over this line until the cardboard started to tear.

He held up the drawing.

Line's gone out, see, he said to Two-Step. I only got to wait for the hook to land.

As a finishing touch, the Prophet drew Two-Step's cowboy hat on his own head.

Rescue II

2014

The Prophet owned a 12-gauge double-barrel shotgun. The only time he'd ever used it was back when he'd had to put Zeke's dog down. He also owned a little derringer, bequeathed to him by an uncle in Mobile. It was this gun that he slid into the front pocket of his loose-fitting khakis. He didn't have any bullets. If he did he wouldn't put them in. The little cast-iron pan would do what he needed. He did not believe in any kind of killing, not capital punishment, abortion, suicide, or injecting an old person like you were putting an animal to sleep. But he did believe in the right to bear arms. The government was not to be trusted. It was a truth he felt up and down his spine. No one in the government besides the president could be trusted. And when the Big Fish—the girl—took his visions to Washington, that same government would stand with their mouths agape. Wisdom and warning from the mouth of a child. They would shun their own duplicity and get to work. They would *home in*.

It was the third Tuesday in April. He drove to Flintstone and parked in a thick hedge of privet a hundred yards behind the Pure station. Beyond the privet were some woods, the private property of a for-rent cabin no one ever rented. Beyond that was a dirt road that ran along the base of the mountain for a few miles, eventually circling back to Nickajack Road.

Twice this week he'd come down to make sure he had the lay of things, walking off the distance between the station and restroom, the restroom and his van. Now he took the cast-iron pan from beneath his seat and stepped out of the car, making sure to leave the keys in the ignition and the passenger door cracked. He went into the restroom and stepped inside the stall. The toilet was filled with shit and cigarette butts with a swollen tampon sitting on top. Flies buzzing everywhere. He set the pan on the tank and tied his bandana around his mouth and nose and sat on the lid, pulling his legs up so his feet didn't show. Above the toilet, just below the ceiling, was a narrow screen through which he could hear birdsong and, in the distance, traffic out on the highway. He'd be able to hear the car pull up when it came. Let it come, Lord, he said aloud. He pulled his legs tight to his chest and felt his heart shoving against them. He cleared his throat and practiced coughing softly into his bandana. In his pocket was a flask with lemon and sugar in some water. Soon as he heard them coming he'd take a swig. He wouldn't need to be quiet for very long. Just a few seconds and it would be done with.

He waited. From time to time he rested his forehead on his knees and closed his eyes. He worried he might doze off. But a cough would come on or a wave of stench would hit, and he'd jolt upright. On the metal stall door, which hung by one hinge so its bottom corner rested on the ground, was a painting of a smiling monkey with a skull tucked beneath his arm, the artist's signature on his foot. Above the urinal the same artist had painted an eyeball the size of a platter, with a rainbow burst in its center. First time he'd come in here he'd been surprised by the graffiti—not that it was here, but how good it was. Used to be graffiti was cusswords and gang signs. Here was a real painter who cared how a thing looked.

He figured he'd been waiting near an hour when he heard the crunch of tires. A car door slammed. A man's voice, and a woman's.

He took a swig and put the flask back in his pocket. Slowly, he lifted the frying pan.

An old man with skinny cricket legs in a shit-stink bathroom, holding the pan he fried potatoes in. He thought of Zeke and his big truck, he thought of Sullivan, and he began to feel nervous. Maybe this was foolish. Not the rescue itself. The way he was going about it. The voices were louder. He'd just sit quietly with his legs tucked up and hope they didn't see him. If they did, he'd pretend he was confused. A crazy old man in the wrong restroom.

He'd go home and think up a better plan.

Two sets of shoes appeared in the opening beneath the stall: black unlaced high-tops, and pink high-heeled sandals. Little red-painted toenails.

Take them all baby that's good.

I know.

You'll be glad for them when you—

I know I know I know.

High and dreamlike and filled with breath! A voice like that would never come from another soul in the world.

He lowered his feet to the floor.

After you're done King'll take you to that movie he promised—

The Prophet stepped out of the stall. The woman was much younger than he'd thought, with acne on her cheeks—but before she could make a sound he hit her on the side of the head with the pan. Once, twice. He tried not to hit too hard, just enough to knock her out. The woman fell and lay face down on the concrete.

The girl looked at the woman, and then at the Prophet.

You're just an old man, she said in her singsongy voice.

He set the pan down and wrapped the girl in a backward hug, covering her mouth with his hand.

Quiet, he said into her ear. If we're both real quiet, we can get you—

But the girl was struggling. He hadn't planned on any struggle. When he'd played it out in his head, the girl had run alongside him through the brush all the way to his van. Big Fish Walking! But she was bucking against him, kicking and hitting at his crotch. He held on to her with one arm and reached to get the derringer out of his pocket. She bit into his finger and he nearly cried out, but he managed to keep his hand over her mouth while he pushed the pistol into her low back.

I'm not going to hurt you, he said. This is a rescue, see?

The girl went limp. Her head flopped back on his shoulder. Maybe she passed out or maybe she was trying to trick him; either way, he was going to have to carry her. He took a few steps but her shoes made a scraping sound on the cement. If he dragged her this way the shoes would leave marks in the dirt, and when the man realized how long the woman and the girl were taking in the bathroom, he would come around to find them and see the tracks to where the Prophet had parked. Any minute now he'd come looking.

The girl was even taller than he'd calculated. He turned her around, reached beneath her armpits, and got her up over his shoulder. Her stomach was jerking like maybe she was going to puke. He peered outside the bathroom door. The man wasn't in sight. He glanced behind at the woman on the ground—saw the rise and fall of her chest—then grabbed the frying pan and, with the girl over his shoulder, ran in the direction of the van. A lopsided scuff *stump* scuff *stump*. If he could just—he gasped for breath, trying not to cough. Just get her in the car and go. He'd planned to drive around for a long time to confuse things, the girl herself and anyone who might be following. Chickamauga Road to Lee Clarkson, down into Rock Spring and all the way to Lafayette. Take the 193 back to Nickajack Road. Up the mountain, out past Cloudland Canyon and into Mentone. Stop awhile, drink some water and wash up, tell her his plan. Turn around and head back to his cabin, where everything was ready.

He ran as best he could. Just get her in the front seat, lock the doors, drive.

If he could just—

There was his fender! The passenger door, cracked like he'd left it. With his foot he pulled it open and flopped the girl onto the seat. One of her shoes was off. No time to go back and look. He tucked in her legs, closed the door, got in and gunned it toward the trees, the van bumping and heaving on the uneven ground. He glanced at the girl, sprawled with her eyes closed and spit in the corners of her mouth. What pills had they been giving her?

Into the woods. Away from the access road and the Pure station.

He didn't look in the rearview.

For a long time he didn't look anywhere but straight ahead.

By the time he reached Lafayette his heart had stopped pumping so fast. He'd been careful to keep to the speed limit, but now there was no traffic around him. He slowed to twenty and reached behind the seat for the jug of water and took a long swig. Then he switched on the overhead bulb and let himself have a good look at the girl.

Her body was in an L shape, top half draped across the seat, head on the center console, feet on the floor. One of her arms stuck out; the other was pinned beneath her torso. He noticed prints like bruises on the pale inside of her upper arm. Had he done that to her? It wasn't easy getting her into the van the way he'd had to do it. The blond wig hung off the side of her head; the part in her hair was flecked with dandruff, with a few pins along the hairline. He hoped she'd stay asleep. He wished he'd thought to put her in the back, where he'd taken out the seats and nailed up paintings to cover the van's sides and ceiling. She might've slept more peacefully lying flat. She might've liked to look at the paintings. He was eager to get her back to the cabin. He'd pushed his own mattress into the corner beside the back door where there were no windows. From there it would be easy for her to get out to use the toilet, or to hide out back if visitors stopped by. For privacy he'd hung two flannel sheets from the

ceiling, boxing out a little room. The sheets were from a
yard sale, king size, light blue with tiny red roses. When
he'd got the sheets hung, he laid down in the makeshift
room to get her vantage. The roses made the other two
walls look empty, so he hung the framed donkey visions
beside the mattress. There were three donkey paintings
but the frames had come in a set of four, so he went
ahead and hung the empty frame, too. Any day now, he
felt, the fourth donkey would show up.

For himself he'd got a blow-up raft at a yard sale, the
kind for a swimming pool. It was shaped like a cactus,
wide enough for two people, with drink holders in the
cactus arms. At first he thought he'd let the air out each
morning, roll it up, and hide it in a cupboard during the
day. That way visitors wouldn't ask why he'd taken to
sleeping on a cactus. But blowing it up took so long he'd
decided to leave it. If anyone asked he'd say it was for
a project. His plan for the girl, if a visitor came, was to
have her hide in the chicken shed. The hens laid their eggs
in old dresser drawers set up on the high windowsills.
They didn't lay in winter, and last fall when it rained
the smell got so bad, he'd thought about just cutting off
their heads and cooking up the meat. Now he was glad
he'd kept them. The girl would have fresh eggs.

Twilight. He didn't know how long he'd been
driving.

Time enough.

He turned the van around.

In the brief lights of small towns he kept glancing at the girl. He noticed a ring of stars tattooed just below her ear, which had hoops and beads going up the side. The Prophet didn't like tattoos or piercings but he did like stars. When God looked down at the planet, he was seeing what people saw when they looked up: darkness, with a few brave lights trembling here and there. The darkness was evil and the lights were God's children staking a claim.

He began to wind up Nickajack. He knew all the curves where the police waited, and he made sure to keep to the speed limit. At the top he took Burkhalter Gap down to Trenton, off the back side of the mountain. That wasn't his original plan, but now that he was up here, he didn't feel like going all the way out to Mentone. Halfway down his gas light blinked on. He hadn't been paying attention to the gauge.

In Trenton he pulled into the station at the back of the Ingles parking lot and turned off the ignition. The girl stirred. He noticed he'd forgotten to put the seat belt on her. He reached over to pull it across and her eyelids flicked open.

Hello, the Prophet said. I seen you weren't able to come to me. So I came to you.

She was blinking fast—in the orangey light he could see her eyes were the color of light-green bottle glass—and then she sat up, put her head down to the floor and vomited.

That'll clean, the Prophet said.

Where am I? the girl said.

The way she was looking at him told him to start the car.

Dayton, he said, pushing on the gas.

The girl was grabbing at her neck like she might strangle herself. He reached over, meaning to put a hand on her shoulder, but she punched him, hard, in his temple. Her knuckles were sharp and his eyes watered. She was pulling at the door handle, fumbling around for the lock. He pushed the gas pedal all the way down and silently asked the Lord to fill the tank.

Where are you taking me? she asked.

A safe place, he said. Where that man and woman can't find you.

You killed Jessamine, she said.

Course I didn't, he said. I only knocked her out a little while.

The girl was crying. He couldn't understand it. He thought she'd just say thank you, thank you. She pulled her knees up to her chest and put them down again, clutching at her throat.

There's a blanket on the floor there behind you, he said. You feel sick again, you throw up into that. Listen. I seen that man hit you. You said, Help me.

For the first time the girl really looked at him. Her mouth was open enough for him to see how her two front teeth hung lower than the rest, how the bottom teeth crowded all together.

You were in the fence, she said.

I been watching you a while, he said.

I don't need help. I need the pills Jessamine has.

We'll be there soon, he said.

Where?

My place.

Shit, she said. Shit, shit, shit.

What's your name?

Ecstasy. Baby Doll. Delicious. Whatever you want to call me.

I don't mean to call you any them kind of names, he said. How old are you?

Eighteen. Twenty-one. Twenty-six.

You don't want to tell me, that's okay. You want to know who I am?

I already know. A john like the rest.

Who I am, he said, is a prophet of the Lord God Almighty!

He didn't mean for it to come out so loud.

Listen, he said, trying to gentle up his voice. I seen them ties on your wrists. I believe they been selling you like a slave.

It's just Backpage, she said. High-end clients. Are you turning me in?

Course not, he said. I got a different plan.

The girl was arching her back and moving her jaw around. She turned to look behind her.

I painted all them, he said. Look, there above you. That's Ghost Jesus in the fiery furnace.

The girl tipped her head back to look.

It was one of his best paintings, was why he nailed it above the passenger seat. He'd covered an old roof shingle in a pink bubble gum color and in the center painted the shape of a man in a long white cloak. He used his fingers to make red and orange and yellow swirls for licks of fire around the body. He planned on swirls of blue, too, to show how a kind of coolness protected the man from burning, but once he'd laid on the first swirl of turquoise, he realized the blue was a mistake. The single turquoise swirl looked like a jewel sitting on Jesus's shoulder. It was his favorite thing about the painting.

Ghost Jesus is the one takes me by the hair and lifts me, the Prophet said, so I can watch myself like someone up on a stage. Ghost Jesus takes me all around the Earth . . .

The girl had turned her whole body to face him. Her expression was different. It was like he'd been seeing her through a husk and something he'd said had shucked it off.

That floating up and watching yourself, she said. I can do that, too.

Platinum Snail Shell

2012

The sickness had started with a tickling in his chest. He swallowed water and cleared his throat but no matter how many times he hacked and spit, there it was again, the itchy urge to cough something up. One day Mae Thomas, the midwife, stopped by. She'd brought him some paints and a bag of apples. Before he could thank her he was taken by a fit. He covered his mouth with his bandana and when he pulled it away Mae's hand flew to her chest.

Just a dry throat, he said.

Three days later she came back and told him get into her car. She said she was taking him down to Chattanooga so a machine could make pictures of his insides.

July on the mountain, thick blankets of kudzu thrown over boulders and spilling down cliffs. On the way down Ochs Highway the leafed-out trees mostly blocked the view of the city, but in places where they thinned he glimpsed the towers out near the dam. Cooling towers, Zeke had called them—but the Prophet had seen something like them in a vision years ago, when Zeke was a baby. It was the only vision he'd never been able to paint. Two beehives, two wars, two sets of bee soldiers swarming out. *We're going to sting 'em to death, sting 'em to death, sting 'em to death*, sang the bees. They flew straight up through the clouds and into outer space.

You do not know what it is you're going to fight! the Prophet said aloud.

Mae reached over and touched his arm. Try not to worry, she said.

He clasped his hands together and placed them in his lap.

The doctor was a young woman with her hair tied back and clear braces on her teeth. She showed him his insides on a big computer screen. Thish is the trachea. The braces made her words sound funny. And here we have the aorta, and the heart. The right lung, which is healthy. And here, on the left—the arrow moved over a patch of light—is the mash.

The Prophet put his face close to the screen. White blocks of lit-up spine stacked orderly on top of each other, see-through gray-white ribs fragile as feathers— and there, to the side of the ribs, was a platinum snail shell, spiraling, throwing out threads. There were his neck and jaw, there were his lips! You couldn't see the abscess. All the uglinesses in him were gone, the body under his body was beautiful as a clear night in winter, the Milky Way brush-swiped above his cabin, powdered with stars.

Longevity, the doctor was saying. Quality of life, immediate family.

Looka here, the Prophet said. Something this beautiful can only be of the Lord.

Our best guess is asbestos exposure, the doctor said. Mae tells me you worked at the old foundry on Broad Street, back during Vietnam?

Seventeen years, he said. I led a team. Knew how to keep the boys in line.

We've seen a number of foundry cases, the doctor said. Asbestos in the laggings, insulation, sand molds, cupolas, and ladles. Even the gloves and aprons. There's a class action lawsuit to help victims offset medical expenses.

Who're they suing? the Prophet asked.

The United States government, I suppose, the doctor said.

I don't want the government looking at my insides, he said.

The doctor walked the Prophet and Mae Thomas down the hall to a cubicle where a man in a suit talked about the costs of treatment options, and how instead of these treatments the Prophet could sign papers choosing to go home and let things take their course. The man looked mostly at his computer while he talked. Every now and then he'd glance at the Prophet and shift in his seat like he was sitting on something painful and trying to ignore it.

Looka here, the Prophet kept saying. Looka here.

On the way home Mae Thomas called Zeke on her cellular phone. The Prophet listened to her tell his son about the snail shell. Lemme talk to him, the Prophet said. But when he heard Zeke saying, Hey, Pop, Pop, you there? he gave the phone back and didn't speak the rest of the way home.

A week later Mae's son Daniel pulled into his driveway. He said he was heading down to the junkyard, that someone had left a pile of beautiful windows with beveled glass, and maybe he'd like to come pick out a few? The Prophet liked painting on glass. On a pane of glass you could see a vision forward and backward. He got in the truck. At the bottom of the mountain Daniel turned the wrong way.

Let's get us some lunch first, Daniel said.

He drove down Broad Street and pulled into the KFC parking lot, where the Prophet saw his son standing beside a red truck with four doors and oversized tires. He hadn't seen Zeke in six years, not since the day he drove to Nashville to see his newborn grandbaby. Zeke wore an unbuttoned flannel over a plain white undershirt. His gut had grown enormous. The hair was gone from his forehead.

Daniel pulled up beside Zeke and rolled down the windows.

Hey there, Pop, Zeke said. He said it like six years was last week.

The Prophet turned to Daniel.

Didn't think you and your mama was equal to tricking an old man, he said.

I got to get back to work, Daniel said.

The Prophet got into Zeke's truck, which was idling noisily. In the back seat were a booster chair and some naked Barbie dolls.

Zeke got in behind the wheel.

How're you feeling? Zeke asked.

Feel like I always feel, the Prophet said. How old's my grandbaby now?

He knew the answer but wanted Zeke to say it.

Sully's six, Zeke said.

A cellular phone sat on the dashboard. Zeke laid a thumb on it and a girl in a collared shirt with a crest appeared. She was smiling, her long brown hair in pigtails. Her front teeth were missing; the Prophet could see the gray-white stubs of the new ones coming in.

We've got her in a good private school, Zeke said. She's reading chapter books already, if you can believe.

Got yourself a nice truck here, the Prophet said. He was angry with his son for tricking him—for not coming home to visit all these years—and he meant to stay that way. But beneath the anger was a kind of excitement. He felt as if he'd just received some good news. It was the way he felt when a crop he'd planted threw up thick hardy sprouts, or when a tourist paid him cash for one of his drawings. He was proud that Zeke owned such a vehicle and sent his daughter to a school you had to pay for, proud that his son—his!—had grown up to manage such things. He reminded himself that the truck and private school were part of a corrupt system of greedy money mongers with their pig snouts mucking around in the troughs of the workingman. He looked at the dashboard with its fancy lights and cellular phone in its holder, he looked up at the movie screen in the ceiling and the naked dolls littering the back seat and floor, and he tried to ignore the being-proud feeling. All size and no modesty. That was the problem with America. It wasn't enough to just drive somewhere, you had to make a big show and a lot of noise doing it.

Zeke turned onto the freeway that cut through Missionary Ridge.

I know it's been a while since I've been down here, Zeke said. They got me traveling all over the country. I wish you'd let me get you a cell phone.

So the government can keep track of me from their outer space radio towers? the Prophet said. So them politician spies can watch me the way they watch everyone else, walking around half-asleep with their thumbs stuck on pins?

You're free to think about it that way, Zeke said. I'm free to think about it my way. That's the great thing about living in America.

Look, we got to get the visions to the White House, the Prophet said. Bee soldiers need to know what the government is sending them to fight.

Zeke's face had gone red; his fingers opened and closed around the steering wheel.

Never could understand why you want to warn the government about something you think the government itself is involved in, Zeke said.

Big Fish will tell the president, the Prophet said. President's different than the rest of the government.

I guess you figure on him getting reelected, Zeke said.

No question, the Prophet said.

Zeke turned up the radio and they didn't talk anymore. They pulled off at Gunbarrel Road and parked in front of a four-stories-high building. The Prophet realized it was the same place they took his wife when she had the cancer in her breasts. On the outside it was like he remembered but inside the waiting room they'd built a rock fountain in the corner, and instead of hard chairs there were leather couches, and lamps with cloth shades. At the front desk Zeke signed papers saying he would be the one in charge of paying for whatever they were going to do to him, and that he would be the one to make decisions on his behalf. A nurse took the Prophet into a back room with a row of curtained-off chairs. She led him to one of them, closed the curtain, and said to make himself comfortable. She showed him how to recline, settled some cushioned headphones over his ears, then handed him a laminated menu: EDM, R&B, Lo-Fi. He pointed to the only category he recognized: Classic Rock. She set a curved stainless bowl in his lap, cleaned a spot on his arm, stuck a needle in, and wrapped some tape around—there was singing inside his head, something about summer nights—he felt a warm liquid going into him and right then he threw up.

The way he understood it he was supposed to sit here and let this happen twice a week for twelve weeks until the shell didn't send out any more satellites, and then he would have to drink something to light up the shell so a different machine could fire poison at it to make it shrink some more; and after that, if it was small enough, they would cut him open and take out whatever was left. He thought of his wife and the way she shrank up after they took her breasts, how the muscles burnt off her bones till what was underneath her skin was the only thing you could think about when you looked at her. He took off the headphones.

I got my own ideas about this here snail shell, he told the nurse. He began to rip the tape off his arm. She put a hand on his shoulder.

Relax, she said. I'll get your son.

Zeke stood with his hands in his jeans pockets, his eyes looking above the Prophet's head. You got to do what they tell you, Pop, he said. Beneath Zeke's man face was the boy the Prophet remembered.

Gimme them damn papers to sign, the Prophet said.

In another room, a different nurse gave him some prescription papers and an oxygen tank on wheels. The tank had a hose coming out with tubes he was supposed to wear up in his nose.

Them baby wheels can't handle no potato patch, he told the nurse.

She placed the tubes inside his nostrils and told him to breathe. He felt a cold sweet rush of air and yanked the tubes out.

The sun was beginning to set by the time they drove home. The Prophet told Zeke how three people had been cured of alcoholism and one of syphilis just from him singing the mulberry tree song. He told how he would sing it to himself to stop the shell from throwing out threads.

Goddammit, Zeke said. Those things would've happened no matter what.

It wasn't Zeke selling out to the money mongers that bothered him. It wasn't the thought of his son feeling sorry for him. It was that his son hadn't changed since the day he left with the bigwigs. *Your father is sick*, the bigwigs had told him, *his brain saturated with drink for too many years*. It was true. He used to be a regular devil like the rest. Blind and deaf and dumb. But he hadn't touched a bottle since Zeke was born. Thirty-one years, not a drop on the tongue.

Thirty-one years not a drop, he said aloud.

I can't take care of you, Zeke said. I've got my wife and baby girl. I've got my job.

You hear me asking?

It'll be like when Mom died. You can't take care of yourself when it gets that way.

Zeke had his face turned away. The Prophet hadn't seen his son cry since he was eight years old. Zeke's dog had left a fresh squirrel carcass near the porch steps; two weeks later he'd heard his wife yelling and ran in from the field to see blood on Zeke's arm and the dog backed up against the wall of the trailer, snarling. He kicked the dog out the front door and took the shotgun off its pegs. Stay inside, he told Zeke. He closed the door behind him. The dog was on the porch, twisting around like something was biting everyplace on his body. With his boot he shoved the animal off the porch—it bolted up the driveway, torso twisting like a caught fish—took aim and put a slug into its head. The Prophet turned to see his son behind him.

That dog was already dead, he'd said to Zeke. Died the minute it ate that squirrel.

Zeke had opened his mouth and let the sound come out.

Now, in the truck, he glanced over at his son's arm to see the scar. But Zeke's sleeves were rolled down.

At the top of Ochs Highway Zeke cracked the windows. They drove in silence past the fancy neighborhood with the stone gates at the entrance, past the Living

Waters Assemblies of God and the AME and Baptist churches, past the fire station and the road down to Trenton. Lightning bugs glittered in the roadside ditches. Buzz-saw cicadas, tree frogs like music boxes winding up. They turned onto the dirt road beside the mailbox shaped like a bear holding a honeycomb.

The Prophet couldn't remember the last time he'd felt this happy. His son was coming home. He would show him all the things he'd done to the place. The recent paintings, the Ezekiel machine he'd started to build; the pipe he'd installed on the woodstove, the new stainless rain barrel; the soft earth of his potato patch and neat rows of beans and squash. His son would see how well he'd been doing on his own.

When they reached the cabin Zeke put the truck into park. He didn't get out.

You see my new sign out there? the Prophet said. The Watchman. Like in Isaiah. Watchman, what time of the night. I plan to get some reflecting tape to lay on top of the letters—

I need to get back, Zeke said. Here, I brought something for you.

It was a cellular phone. Zeke pressed his thumb and the screen lit up. For a few minutes he tapped around on the screen.

Shit, Zeke said. You'll have to drive to Hinkles to get a signal.

I'm not getting put to sleep by one of them spy towers dressed up like a tree, the Prophet said.

Zeke explained how to use the cellular but the Prophet paid no attention. His son slid the phone and the box it came in inside the bag with pills from the pharmacy.

Come on inside a minute, the Prophet said. Get you some beans and peanuts.

I got plenty of food, Pop, Zeke said.

You got it now but wait: soon you'll be wishing you would've took it.

Again Zeke looked away. The Prophet laid a hand on his son's shoulder—he meant to speak a blessing over him—but Zeke shoved it off.

There's something I should've said to you a long time ago, Zeke said, so I'll say it now: I'd come around more if you'd only take me for who I am.

The words were like guitar strings wound too tight.

The Prophet stepped out of the truck. Zeke carried the oxygen tank up the porch steps, set it beside the front door, and got back in the car. The Prophet watched his son back up and turn around. Taillights flickering between the trees. Zeke's arm came out the window and gave a short wave before the car disappeared. The Prophet waved back. He would speak a blessing anyhow. Something protective about Zeke and his wife and child. Lord, Lord, he began. It was all he could think to say.

Her Fingers on His Art

2014

The Prophet knew a seizure was coming on by the way the girl's eyes would suddenly widen and stare someplace far-off, like someone said Don't blink or I'll shoot. Then her arms would stretch out stiff and her fingers press together into claw shapes. The first time this happened he ran to the kitchen to get a wet rag and found Two-Step sitting in a haze of smoke, his back against a cupboard.

See what's a-happening to her, Two-Step said. *And you thought you was rescuing.*

Fiend, he said. I'll deal with you later.

He went back and tucked the rag into the girl's mouth and pinned down her arms while the whites of her eyes yanked into her skull to the beat of some internal rhythm. Click, click, click.

You can't save her, Two-Step cried. *You ain't a doctor and you won't take her to one and when she dies it'll be your fault!*

But he'd seen withdrawal before. Meth heads with their tin cans and lit rocks, smack addicts who went from snorting to smoking to needles. He'd gone through it himself after he cold-turkeyed the Jack Daniel's. The shakes and sweats, nightmares, never able to sleep more than an hour at a time—it was just what happened to a body coming off whatever poisons were polluting its blood. He knew to keep her head propped and made sure she didn't choke on her tongue while she jerked and clawed at her legs. He could tell her nails were cheap stick-ons. When she was quiet he asked if he could peel them off. She nodded. He chucked the bits of plastic into the woodstove.

He gave her privacy when she slept. Helped her clean up after the diarrhea and vomit. He had some of his wife's old clothes and underthings washed and laid out for her, and a stack of clean towels. She let him do anything to help her as long as he moved slowly and gently. She'd thrashed and fought him so much during the rescue, he figured that was her nature. Now here she was, limp and compliant, speaking only single words. Yes, water; no, food. He found himself wishing she had more fight in her.

The girl's eyes watered and snot tinged with blood came out of her nostrils. In between seizures she either slept or stared at the ceiling. Sometimes she was so still he reached to feel for the pulse fluttering her neck cords. Often in her sleep the girl shook her head and cried out, and when she did this he'd get his guitar and sit beside

her and sing the healing song until she quieted. He fed
her sips of water with a plastic spoon and made sure to
keep talking to her, even if she didn't respond.

You are suffering like Christ, he'd say. Christ had
to go to a place farther inside the garden than any of
his friends could go. His friends went to sleep on him,
but I won't.

You can't help her, Two-Step said.

There's nothing to do but just get through it, he said
to the girl, ignoring Two-Step. He spoke tenderly, the
way he might speak to his granddaughter. He wished
Zeke would tell Sullivan about him. He wanted the child
to know she had a grandfather in Alabama who could
walk around behind the world's curtain, then come back
and paint what he saw.

He tried to keep himself awake with the painting.
Often he fell asleep with a brush in his hand.

By the fourth day the girl was holding down larger
amounts of water. He set a full jug beside her bed and a
can of Coca-Cola with a plastic straw and left her alone
for an hour. When he came back the Coke was gone
and she was sleeping peacefully. He put out two more
cans, and a packet of orange crackers with peanut butter
sandwiched inside.

Kidnapping a child and keeping her hostage, Two-
Step said. *You think this story ends anywhere but prison?*

He wasn't keeping her hostage. She was free to go
soon as she was well. He'd told her so over and over.

When you're feeling better, he said, if you want to leave, I will take you anywhere you want to go. But I'm a-hoping you'll want to stay awhile.

With the girl here Two-Step was doubling down. Which proved something. Two-Step wouldn't be trying so hard if the girl wasn't the Big Fish.

The Prophet had gone to see a tent revival preacher once, back in the days he worked at the foundry. The preacher had paced back and forth in front of a packed audience. After the sermon people formed a line to come up on stage. One by one, the preacher slashed an X into the air in front of them; one by one, they fell over backward. The Prophet would be like that preacher. He saw himself and Two-Step up on a stage, about to do hand-to-hand combat. Two-Step would throw down his hat and make ready to punch. It was then the Prophet would make the giant X and say, *In the name of Jesus I command you!* Twice now he'd come at Two-Step with the intention of making the X. Both times he'd found only drifting smoke and a pocket of stale air. Like him deciding to fight was what made Two-Step disappear.

Coward, he said aloud. He wasn't sure if he meant Two-Step or himself.

The fourth night the girl slept peacefully. When the coughing took him he went out to the porch so as not to wake her. The sky was starless, blank as fog. He sat in his rocker and drifted in and out of sleep. He dreamt the girl showed him the cats she'd owned as a child. The creatures crawled up his legs, pocking his thighs with their claws. They clung to his shoulders and purred in his ears and licked his face, their fur stuffing his mouth and filling his throat.

He woke to an overcast morning, the air heavy with humidity. Inside, the girl was still asleep. She thrashed so much the first night he'd taken the sheets off the mattress and laid out some towels. Now he saw she'd piled the towels at the foot of her mattress and lay on the sheet. Both Coke cans were empty, the crackers gone. There was urine in the bucket beside her bed. He was glad she figured to use it.

Five days. Likely the poisons were flushed. Now she'd need to get up her strength, eat some real food. He wanted to show her the outhouse and creek, and the chickens.

He got the food-scrap bucket and walked across his field to the clearing just past the tree line. It was here that he and Zeke had built the shed. He thought it would be a good place to stockpile food but he'd ended up using it to store things he brought up from the junkyard. Windows and doors, old fireplace mantels, saw blades, car parts. Two years ago a visitor brought him sixteen pullets in exchange for a winter's worth of canned tomatoes. He'd hauled the junk back to the cabin and repurposed the shed as a coop.

He looked out to where the ridges swelled up before they flattened into Nashville. Dark clouds billowing up overtop of lighter ones. Too warm for late April. He hoped it would storm, a nice thick rain to cool things off.

In the coop the chickens were roosting up on the sills. I got someone for you to meet today, he said to them. The chickens footed down the two-by-four, lifting their wings to air out their armpits. He scattered potato skins and rotting soybeans and lettuce, then stood on the overturned bucket to reach for the eggs, wincing. For the first time in a while he thought of the oxygen tank in the corner, hidden behind the rakes and pitchforks and shovels. After Zeke had left he'd dragged the tank out here. He'd thrown out the empty phone box but put the phone itself inside the bag with the pills and stuffed it to the bottom of the feed bin. He didn't want those things in his cabin, reminding him of when they tried to put the medicine in his arm. The last day he'd seen his son.

There were four eggs this morning, soft, one with a near-transparent shell. There was something he was supposed to add to their feed when eggs came out like this. He couldn't remember what. Maybe the girl would like to take care of the chickens. He could show her how to change out the nesting boxes and rake up the shit for fertilizer, explain how if you didn't wash the eggs they'd keep longer.

Back in the cabin he propped open both doors so that a current of air puffed and lowered the shirts hung over the windows. He chunked up the fire and put three small potatoes in a pot to boil, then got out his paint and brushes. He planned to make a bush bloomed out with flowers. But when he sat in front of the section of wall he intended to paint, immediately he began to cough. He spat into his bandana and wadded it up without looking.

He'd lie on his side for a minute, let his chest settle. Then he'd get to work.

He woke to a scratching sound and the smell of something burnt. A strong wind sent dried corn husks scraping across the floor. He dragged himself to standing and saw the potatoes had charred to black. The girl's curtains were pushed aside, and she was there, sitting cross-legged with her back to him.

Something like happiness, liquid, shot up into his chest.

She'd changed into a pair of gray sweatpants and a T-shirt. Through the fabric he could see the sharp nubs of her spine. Her hair was tied up into a knot; at the nape of her neck, just below the hairline, was a tattoo of a crown.

Well, look at you, he said to the girl. You must be feeling better.

She turned to face him. Even with the sunken-in cheeks and dark circles her face was softer, her features more arranged. She tried to stand and sat again.

You've come through it all right, he said. Worst part's over.

It smells disgusting in here, she said.

Beneath the burnt smell was the stink of the towels and wadded up clothes. He needed to show her the way down to the creek. He pulled the scorched potatoes off the fire and dumped them in the scrap bucket, then closed the front and back doors.

We're in the mountains, aren't we, she said.

It's safe here, he said. That man and woman won't be able to find you.

A shadowy expression passed quickly across her face.

Manager, she said. And foster sister. The one you killed.

Couldn't hit hard enough to kill anyone even if I tried, he said.

The girl stood and took a few shaky steps in her bare feet. Again the Prophet thought how tall she was—five seven, five eight. Nearly tall as himself.

I'd like to use your phone, please, she said.

Don't have one, he said.

Take me back, she said.

Back where?

Macon. Where my manager is.

What he wanted to say was: What kind of manager punched a child? What kind of manager gave a child them pills and made her do what she'd done? He didn't understand it. She'd reached for the light when he flashed. He'd seen her lips saying, *Help me.* He needed to get her focused on the here and now. Tell her she was chosen by God for an important job.

Sure I'll take you, he said. But you need to eat first. Get some real food in your system. You like eggs?

And then you'll take me down the mountain?

He swallowed.

Long as you're holding down the food, s'pose I will, he said.

This seemed to satisfy her. She went back to sit on the mattress.

I thought I dreamed those, she said, pointing to the donkeys.

Hung 'em there for you, he said. So you'd have something nice to look at.

Are they horses?

Everything in his life till now—the visions, his wife and the breast cancer, Zeke and Sullivan—all of it rushed together behind him to form a road that brought him here, to this moment. What he was about to say was of eternal significance.

Something the size of a quarter and heavy as a dictionary sat on his tongue. With effort he thrust it between his lips.

The one with wings, he said. That's Celebrating Donkey. He flies all over the planet! Next is Bags-of-Trouble Donkey. Third is Big-Tears. One more's coming, is why there's an empty frame.

As he spoke, the girl touched each painting with a finger the way she'd touched the window when he flashed the light.

What do you mean, coming? she asked.

The weight on his tongue. The smell of smoke, different from the charred potatoes.

Tell her about the movie screen, Two-Step said.

The idea, he said. I'm a-waiting for an *idea*, see. And when the idea comes, I go on and paint it.

Taking the glory all for yourself!

The Prophet went to the kitchen and cracked the four eggs into the charred frying pan. From the corner of his eye he saw Two-Step jigging in place, thumbs in his belt loops, hat pulled low.

Taking, the glory, all for, yourself.

Furiously he stirred.

The girl was walking around the cabin now, looking at the vines and the clotted-paint orange-and-yellow centers of flowers. He watched her run her fingers over the beans and bits of broken glass in the eleventh-hour clock; saw her touch the nose of the papier-mâché pig with the roll of toilet paper in its mouth. She stood in front of the snaky lizard pouring out of the Jack Daniel's bottle, tracing her fingers over the beads he'd glued along its tail. He'd used Christmas tree bulbs, red, for the lizard's eyes.

Her fingers on his art.

He dumped the eggs onto a plate and handed it to the girl. She stood there holding it like she was a guest who'd brought him a casserole and didn't know where to put it.

You nearly killed her and now you're trying to poison her with them old eggs.

They're good eggs, he said. Fresh from my chickens.

There's chickens here? she said.

Across the field. I'll show you. Lemme clear you a place.

Around the tree of life he'd built a kind of shelf that doubled as a table. He shoved aside hammers and wrenches and screwdrivers and a pair of plastic goggles with no strap. But the girl sat cross-legged on the floor beside the heap of saw blades, balancing the plate on her lap. He wiped a fork on his pants and handed it to her.

Them blades painted like eyeballs, he said. That's my Ezekiel machine. I need one more blade to make twelve. Then I'll fix it up on the wall with the motor. See here.

He arranged three blades so the teeth of one hooked into the teeth of the next. He spun the first and all three clicked a few turns before coming loose.

I was hunting for the smallest blade when I spotted you, he said. Forgot about searching after that.

For weeks he'd imagined cooking for the girl—feeding her, an angel of God, the holiness of it—so he was surprised by the messy way she ate. She chewed with her mouth open so he could see the liquid eggs moving around between her teeth. He'd cleaned her shit and vomit and urine but this wet smacking was something different. For the first time since the rescue he felt queasy.

He lifted his guitar and sat in his recliner, making a show of tuning the strings.

You were singing, the girl said. The same song, over and over.

"The Sound of A-Going," he said. It's the healing song. I got lots of verses for it.

Jackson said he'd teach me to play guitar, the girl said. Fucking asshole.

I can teach you, he said. He almost said, Who's Jackson? But he stopped himself. *Keep her focused,* he thought. He strummed a few chords, feeling content. Two are better than one: that was a line in the book of Hosea. A cord of three strands is not easily broken. Meaning Hosea plus Gomer plus God himself.

Between bites the girl kept glancing up at him. Somewhere behind her eyes, or maybe inside them, was a cracked-open door: Can I trust you?

He cleared his throat and tried to sing a verse of "Little David Play on Your Harp," but his voice came out thick and scratchy. He couldn't stand the sound of it. He held out the guitar.

You wanna try it? he asked.

She set the plate aside and he laid the instrument across her lap. She ran her fingers back and forth over the open strings, lightly, a sound like wind chimes.

Chords is easy, he said. In a week or two you'll know more songs than—

The girl set the guitar aside and went back to eating.

I make good money, she said. My manager buys me things. I have to pee, and wash. And then you'll take me down the mountain like you promised.

A shard of anger pricked at the edge of his happiness. He reminded himself she was a child. Sixteen, seventeen most. It might take some time for her to understand that what he'd done was save her. That she'd needed saving.

If she wanted to leave on her own that was her business. He wouldn't stop her. He'd drive her to the Shell station, no farther.

He had to make her want to stay.

I'll show you the toilet, he said. Nice cool stream you can wash up in. Put on them rubber boots there. You say you like chickens?

The girl nodded.

I bet that manager never gave you chickens, he said.

America!

2014

The girl followed him down the embankment to the hut with the porcelain toilet over the hole, and when she finished they went all the way down to the pebbly creek beneath the oak trees. The storm clouds had blown off to the north, leaving a blue sky with puffs of gray-white here and there. No rain again. He'd brought along two empty water jugs and made sure the girl brought one as well. She waded out and sat in the flowing water with all her clothes on. It was the first time he'd seen her smile, a half grin, her mouth open and the corners of her eyes pulling up. She had a dimple in one cheek so when she smiled she looked even younger than he guessed she was. She undid the knot on top of her head, and when she lay back in the water her hair spread out like reeds in the current. It outraged him to think what she'd been made to do. Just a child there in the shallows. He coughed and spat and settled himself on a tree root. Soft decay all around. He wished he could lie down in the shade and take a nap. It was getting harder and harder to make his way down here. Going up would be worse.

The girl stepped out of the water and sat on a rock. She was shivering. The wet T-shirt clung to her shape, her collarbones like spindles. He took off his overshirt and set it around her shoulders. He should've brought a towel. He should have gotten her some soap, maybe shampoo. He had no idea what a girl might want in the way of beauty products.

You're really alone up here, aren't you, the girl said. Like, no neighbors or anything.

I been up here a long time. Zeke—that's my son—he was twelve when we built the cabin. Over twenty years ago now.

You have kids?

Just Zeke. He lives in Nashville. I used to be married, he added.

He wasn't sure if she'd heard. She was twisting her hair into a rope, wringing out the water.

Where do you get money? she asked. For food and gas or whatever?

Don't need much, he said. People buy vegetables. A few regulars come for the healing song. Don't take no money for that but some leave it anyhow—

But he didn't want to talk about himself.

What's your name? he said. I mean the real one you was given as a baby.

Michael, she said. It's a boy's name.

King David had a wife named Michael. How old are you?

Her chin went up, like she expected him to argue with whatever she was about to say.

It's okay if you don't want to tell me, he said.

I'll be fifteen in August, she said.

The Prophet had to concentrate on keeping the muscles in his face very still.

Sullivan, he managed to say. My grandbaby. She'll be eight in August. You could be her sister.

Immediately he regretted saying the word. He didn't want to remind the girl of that foster sister in the bathroom.

Not *the girl*, he thought. *Michael.*

Michael Michael Michael.

She was looking down at the creek.

It's them pebbles singing, he said. Water playing its own instrument!

I could hear it the whole time, she said.

Then she said—her face was turned away so he wasn't sure if he heard it or only imagined hearing it— Thank you for helping me.

On the way back up to the cabin the Prophet made a decision. When the girl asked him to take her back, he would tell her the truth. I won't stop you from leaving, he'd say. But I won't return you to them criminals.

I got an important job for you to do, he'd say, if only you can trust me a little while.

Two-Step was gone, leaving behind the scent of burnt fish. The smell made the Prophet hungry. He thought he might like to eat some fish. A long time since he'd had a trout on his plate.

The girl changed into jean shorts and a collared shirt with a pineapple on the pocket. Most of the clothes he'd given her had been his wife's, but these he'd found at a yard sale. He'd had to guess on the sizes and was happy to see he hadn't been too far off. She'd tucked the shirt in a way that seemed to be holding up the shorts. He'd have to find her a length of shoestring for a belt.

He asked if she was still hungry and she said yes, so he gave her a jar of peaches and bowl of peanuts. Again, she sat on the floor, cracking the shells. He sat in his recliner and looked around the cabin, trying to see his vision boards the way the girl might. The lower-down paintings were Bible verses he'd painted in different colors. Most were hidden behind old doors and roof shingles and stacked-up buckets of paint.

He got up and with his foot pushed aside a box of dusty gourds. WORD OF THE LORD THAT CAME TO HOSEA SUN OF BERRI DURING THE REIN OF UZZIA JOTAM AHAZ HEZAKIAH KINGS OF JUDA. Ten years since he'd painted that one. Seeing the words gave him an idea—a beautiful idea! He needed to think it through. But here was the girl beside him, reading aloud what he'd painted. She pronounced the hard words without sounding out.

Hoo-whee, he said. Where'd you learn to read like that?

You need to fix *son*, she said.

Not asking him to take her back!

How about you fix it? he said, trying to keep his voice calm and not too excited sounding. Zeke had been around Michael's age when he started to lose interest in the paintings. Seemed like he always had to be somewhere. At the time the Prophet hadn't paid enough attention to the change. He didn't ask Zeke enough questions. His son was busy; that was all. Normal for a boy his age to be working odd jobs and having a social life. It wasn't till the Day of Big Trouble at the country club that he realized how angry Zeke was, how much he'd changed. By then it was too late. There was no bringing him back to the Prophet's way of seeing.

He got a tube of black paint and a brush and also his palette: a piece of cardboard with hardened colors layered up on top of each other. He squeezed out some black and watched as she closed off the *u* to make a lopsided *o*.

How high up in the grades are you? he asked the girl.

She didn't answer. She was twirling the brush around and around in the black paint. Seemed like she was trying to make up her mind about something.

I'm his favorite, she finally said. He'll look for me. When he finds me he'll—

No one'll find you here, he said.

She still had on the boots. His wife's. They were the color of a spruce tree, chalky with use, the decorative side buckles broken and dangling.

Them boots look nice on you, he said.

Why'd you bring me here? she said.

Her eyes on him, the cracked-open door inside them. The rushing-together road.

Eternal significance.

Lemme show you my chickens, he heard himself say.

She followed him across the fallow field. Normally he would've planted the whole thing out by now. This year he'd only managed a few rows of corn and pole beans, some feeble radishes. At the potato patch he stooped and dug around with his fingers and brought up a handful of twisted spuds. Too small. He put them into his pocket anyhow.

The girl blinked in the full sun. He noticed she had a habit of suddenly wrinkling her nose and rubbing at it, violently, with the heel of her palm.

The hens clucked nervously when they stepped into the shed. Michael pulled her shirt over her nose.

You need to rake, she said.

Guess I do, he said. Close them doors or they'll run out. I used to let 'em roam but it was feeding the coyotes, is why I'm down to five.

What are their names? she asked.

They're just chickens, he said, then realized his mistake.

Maybe you'd like to name them, he said.

He showed her the bucket he stood on to gather eggs, and the bin of dried cobs, how to strip the corn with a paint scraper; the old armoire that he'd turned into the feed bin, and the metal watering trough. He'd planned on saying, This where you can hide when visitors come, but that could wait. He hadn't counted on how bad the smell would be. He couldn't imagine undertaking to rake and shovel now. Even talking was an effort. He'd done more talking today than the whole year put together.

He glanced over to the corner with the oxygen tank. Thought again of the pills and the phone at the bottom of the feed bin.

Michael was squatting, tossing out bits of corn. The Rhode Island Red—biggest of the five, tame and slow-witted—stepped toward her with its neck thrusting. In an instant the girl had it upside down and tucked to her side.

I guess you know your way around a chicken, the Prophet said.

Mine was named Chewy, she said. I used to have one for a pet.

That manager let you keep a chicken? he asked.

It was before him, she said. Before everything.

The hen's black eye was fixed on him. The girl was stroking its neck.

I can help you clean up in here, if you want, she said.

The Prophet thought he might collapse from the joy charging his veins.

After dark he lit the lamps and fed the woodstove, then collapsed into his recliner, his face hot but his body taken in waves of shivers.

The girl sliced up the potatoes and fried them with eggs. She seemed at ease with a spatula in her hand. He told her about the barrels of dried beans he'd been meaning to sort, and the jars of tomatoes and peppers and peaches, the drawers full of onions and squash. Told her about the rain barrel, how the gutters fed into it, and the barrel beside the sink, which he tried to keep full of water from the creek.

She brought him a plate and he forced himself to take a few bites. Knife pain in his side, but it didn't matter. Nothing mattered now that she was here.

She started opening his kitchen drawers and cupboards. He'd stopped paying attention to what was in them. Empty bottles and jars, bleach and ant spray and cleaning supplies, dirty plates and bowls, boxes of dried milk and powdered drink mixes, cans of soup. Old appliances he meant to fix up and sell, blenders, handheld mixers, coffee grinders.

You get hungry you help yourself to whatever you want, he said.

He dozed, listening to the clatter of pans and dishes, the clink of silverware and slosh of water. For the first time since the rescue he felt he might be able to sleep a night through. Later—he wasn't sure how late it was—he got up and turned down the lamp wicks. Before lying on his raft he slid the bolts into place on the front and back doors and set the padlocks.

Michael was sitting on her bed, making a stack of old *National Geographic*s for a kind of nightstand.

Here, he said. This key's yours.

He thought about saying good night or sweet dreams—something he might've said to Zeke or to his granddaughter if he'd ever got the chance—but a shyness took him.

He lay on his raft, turning from one side to the other, from his back to his stomach. The knife kept insisting on itself. Eventually he found that if he lay on the side with the knife and tucked himself into a ball shape, the posture created two kinds of counterpressure: the wood floor pressing up through the raft, his own knees pressing into his chest. This position gave him some relief.

Across from him the girl's curtains glowed with pinkish light. The flipping of magazine pages . . . flutter of angel wings . . .

He woke in darkness, coughing. When the fit was over he listened until he heard the girl's gentle snoring. One of his legs had gone numb. He rubbed at it until he felt the limb drag itself back to life. He finished off the water beside him. He needed more but didn't want to risk waking the girl. At least the coughing fit hadn't disturbed her. He sipped air between his lips, trying not to agitate his lungs.

Wide-awake. If only he could light the lamp and paint. Maybe he'd go over his groundwork speech. There were things he needed to explain, to lay the groundwork for the visions, and why they were important. He'd had the speech memorized awhile now. It mostly pieced together things he'd heard on the Christian radio station, the one his wife used to listen to, and from the end-times Pentecostals who visited from Hinkles and Ringgold and Trenton. He used to imagine himself giving the speech to the president. Now, sick as he was, he knew he'd be making the speech just to the girl. He was going to have to adjust it.

America!

That was how his speech began. He didn't want to change that part. He liked how the word introduced his subject and also addressed his audience.

America! We got all this power, see. Power and money and the feeling we got to use it, because we think we been given it by God. Nation's founders said America was God's New Israel. Brought forth out of slavery to a foreign government, just like the Israelites. Crossed the sea just like they done. But the Israelites didn't have money or power, only a real innocence. America's got money and power and the *lie* of innocence. We think God is on our side and whatever we do with our money and power to the people in them countries across the ocean, God will bless it because we're his chosen nation. But I seen different. Our defeat is coming. It's coming from a military no one's laid eyes upon that'll make all the armies of the Earth look like a wasp's nest you could knock off the underside of a porch rail. Warfaring angels—that's what's a-coming. Ten thousand times ten thousand stars dropping from the sky to fight the ancient evil coming up from beneath—

No, too much. It needed to be quieter. More personal to the girl. He tried again:

America! We overcome every crisis and we think it's because we're innocent, and whatever we do with our money and power in them countries across the ocean, God will bless it because we're his chosen nation. God's New Israel. But I seen different. Jesus said to watch for the signs of the End like you'd watch a fig tree come into bloom. You're one of the signs, Michael, what's been done to you is part of the ancient evil on the planet, what warfaring angels are coming down to fight. But if the people will repent, if the armies of the Earth will only lay down their weapons, the Lord will—

Too much, too much!
He tried again:

Jesus said to watch for the signs of the End like you'd watch a fig tree coming into bloom. You're one of the signs, Michael. You asked why I brought you here. Well I got some information about America and I believe you been chosen to take it to the president. But there's another reason. Hosea rescued Gomer from her way of life and took care of her. Them two made a picture for everyone to see the way God loved his people. It's you and me, Michael. We're the remnant. A picture of God's faithfulness to an adulterous nation.

There. That was how he'd tell her.

Six days. How many more would she stay? How many would it take to convince her to leave again? He needed to keep track. In the soft wood of the wall beside him, he used his thumbnail to carve six small lines.

Zeke and the Day of Big Trouble

2003

When Zeke turned twenty-two he got a job working for a construction company down in Chattanooga. Mostly he did finish work. The Prophet told him he should be framing and hanging drywall, but secretly he was proud his son did the trim. How a thing looked was important. Not just *Is it useful?* but *Is it nice to look at?* Trees made fruit, and fruit is useful, he'd said to Zeke. But before fruit comes flowers, and there's not a thing to be done with them but look.

On weekends, his son worked at the country club in Fairyland fixing gym equipment, raking the tennis courts, cleaning up after weddings and high school dances. From down in St. Elmo and Flintstone you could see the back-side of the club like a stucco growth on the side of the cliff. Zeke said the back might be ugly, but the front was a stone castle with a turret. To get to the entrance and valet parking, he said, you had to drive between boulders the size of upended trailers.

I'd like to see them boulders, the Prophet said to Zeke.

Early one Saturday morning, before the club was open, Zeke took him on a tour. They went down a hallway with restrooms and closed office doors and up a spiral staircase into the turret, where there were shelves filled with books and cushioned window benches. Zeke wore a baseball cap and had a wad of chaw in his lower lip. He opened a window and spit.

I like to come up here on my breaks, Zeke said. Look, I want to show you something.

He pulled a book from a shelf and handed it to the Prophet: *A Culinary Guide*.

Chef's been teaching me, Zeke said. How to melt chocolate without burning it, and how to make an omelet, and a sauce called bechamel.

The Prophet flipped some pages. *Langue de Boeuf*, *Napoleons*.

He snapped the book shut.

God gave you the singing gift, the Prophet said.

A person can be good at more than one thing, Zeke said.

They went downstairs to the ballroom, where Zeke showed him the vacuum-looking machine he polished the floor with. He said the chandeliers were supposed to show up in the floor so that when people danced the light would be coming from above and below. The Prophet looked at the shiny dark wood on the walls, the carved-stone fireplaces and the gold chandeliers with jewels dripping down. In the center of the ceiling was a mirrored ball.

These lights is nothing compared to ones I seen Up Yonder, the Prophet said.

Zeke put the polisher back in the closet and went out to the balcony. The Prophet followed. Something wasn't right. He'd only meant to say that he understood about the shining and the lights and how important it was to keep the floors polished.

He stood on the balcony beside Zeke, facing east. It was light out but the sun wasn't above the horizon yet. Pockets of mist like clouds stuck between the ridges, which rippled all the way to the Blue Ridge Mountains. Directly below them was the SEE ROCK CITY barn and the corn maze spelling out COCA-COLA. Off to the left was the big Atlanta–Nashville freeway snaking through the ridge cut and, beyond that, the white concrete mess of downtown Chattanooga. He could see sections of the river between the buildings.

It's a nice view you got, the Prophet said.

It's good at night, too, Zeke said. Zeke's hands on the wrought iron looked puffy. The Prophet pulled up his own jeans and tucked in his shirt. Maybe he should've dressed up a little. He hoped he wouldn't have to meet Zeke's boss.

Them beehives, he said, pointing. I seen them in a vision. Long time ago, when you were a baby. Never been able to paint it.

Zeke squinted. You mean the nuclear plant? he said.

I seen bee soldiers flying out of them hives, the Prophet said. Believing they are the most powerful army in history.

They're cooling towers, Pop, Zeke said.

Look, we got to get this information to the White House—

Beneath his hat Zeke's face was something you'd burn your fingers on if you touched.

Why do you have to turn every goddamn thing into something else? Zeke said.

The Prophet had heard Zeke cuss plenty but not *goddamn*. He licked his lip and reached out but his son backed away.

Things are just things, Pop, Zeke said. Towers are towers. Chandeliers are chandeliers.

Depends how you look, the Prophet said. Onion's just a onion till you slice longwise and see a tongue of fire inside.

Zeke spat over the rail. Yeah, I remember, he said. Every potato covered with the watchful eyes of the Lord.

How'd they get on to food? He meant to tell about the hives.

Listen, the Prophet said. Bad times are coming.

Even if you could get yourself to the White House, Zeke said, not a soul's gonna listen to some crazy old man.

Somewhere beneath the Prophet's ribs a trapdoor opened. He held on to the balcony rail with both hands. On the outside he was standing with Zeke but on the inside he was falling through the trapdoor into a dark place he never knew was there inside his body until now.

I don't believe your goddamn visions, Zeke said. Never have and never will.

Zeke's mouth was smiling but the Prophet could see that it was a put-on, that underneath he was afraid.

Seemed like you was interested, the Prophet said. Seemed like you believed.

Kids believe whatever parents tell them, Zeke said, till they grow up and realize they were tricked.

A blue flash of electricity in his spine. Ungrateful! He never tried to trick Zeke. He'd never tried to trick anyone. He was just telling the truth of what he saw.

What I believe, Zeke said, is that whatever I'm looking at is all there is.

Shoving him down into the trapdoor with his words.

Your mother, the Prophet said, when she was a-laying on the couch—

I know, Zeke said. God's hand punched me in. Miracle baby with a high-and-mighty calling.

His son's body was shaking. It was like a trickle of water came out when Zeke said *crazy old man*, and that trickle opened a bigger crack and let some more water out. Now his body was the wall holding back whatever was trying to burst through.

You need to listen, Zeke said, because I am going to say this only once: what you're seeing is the inside of your own head.

The Prophet's knees folded and he sat cross-legged, bowing so his chin touched his chest. If Zeke would stop pushing him down with the words.

I will never take your paintings anywhere, Zeke said. They're good for nothing but firewood.

The Prophet looked up at a man he didn't recognize.

Two-Step done got to you, he said.

Zeke squatted beside him.

Listen, Pop, he said, I don't want to hurt you. But a lady here at the club told me she bought pumpkins from you last week. Said you told her she was a buzzing mosquito in her husband's ear and that she better stop nagging him or something bad would happen to her grandson. That lady's husband's been dead eight years and she doesn't have a grandson.

What I saw with her was something future, the Prophet said. Two-Step's put gauze over her eyes and stopped up her ears with cotton.

Zeke put his face so close, the Prophet smelled the Copenhagen in his gum. His son's mouth was pulling this way and that, trying to arrange itself.

No such thing as the devil, Zeke said. No such thing as God, either.

For a wild second the Prophet felt he might grab his son's cheeks and kiss him on the forehead, the way he used to do at bedtime.

You'll come around, the Prophet managed to say.

Zeke stood.

Time to go, he said. He held out a hand. The Prophet took it and felt himself pulled to his feet. The sun was up now, sparkling the sweat on Zeke's forehead and cheeks.

The Prophet put his hands on his son's shoulders.

Listen, he said. You'll come around.

His Announcement Board

2014

A week since the rescue. Any day the girl could've asked him to take her back. Seemed like she wanted to stay.

Only once did he wake to find her crouched beside him, untying the shoestring in his belt loops. He shoved her away.

Never again, he said. You ain't made for that.

It's my job. You're supposed to pay me.

You got a different job to do, is why you're here.

What job?

Just wait awhile longer and I'll tell you, he said.

On day eight he gave her a bandana to tie over her nose and mouth and together they went out to the shed. Mornings were his best time, the pain still dull enough to bear it. He meant to help her rake and shovel, but after lifting a few forkfuls into the wheelbarrow he leaned against a tree while the girl wheeled chicken dung from the coop out to the field and dumped it on his few rows of vegetables. When she finished, she collected the eggs, six of them. He noticed she moved in fits and starts: fast and with purpose one minute, sitting and staring into the distance the next. If he hadn't've known better he might've said that in those quiet moments she was meditating.

Later that day he showed her his tomato starts, explaining how to fill the hanging baskets with loose dirt from the potato patch. He showed her how deep to plant, and how to loosen up the root ball without ripping apart the tangled threads. She seemed happy to have her hands in the dirt. He'd thought he would've told her his plan by now. He hadn't counted on how long the withdrawal would take, or how interested she'd be in things like chickens and spelling words. He hadn't counted on her being able to read the way she could.

Nine days, ten. Chores in the mornings, rest in the afternoons. Evenings, he was too worn out to do anything but lie back in his recliner. The girl opened jars of fruit and fried up eggs on top of the woodstove. He forced himself to take bites while she looked at old magazines. She'd taken to the painting. He'd shown her how to mix up colors; how to lay on paint to make a base, and, when it dried, to layer up the images. The vines began to grow, spooling out over the walls and in between the vision boards, twisting up to the ceiling. She especially liked to paint flowers. Her petals were spokes in sun yellow, coral, amethyst, blueberry, parrot green.

Eleven days, twelve.

He'd thought the happiest years of his life were behind him. The good years with Zeke in the cabin. With Zeke his happiness had been simple, full of bright angles and either-or questions. What he felt with the girl around was different. A light breeze was always coming off her, ruffling up whatever he'd decided in his head. *Today's the day*, he'd tell himself when he woke. *Groundwork speech. Tell her she's the Big Fish.* Then he'd say Good morning, Michael, the little wind would froth up around her, and he'd forget all about his plan. It was like each night he went to bed meaning to climb a hill the next day. Then he'd wake and find himself already at the top, a flat grassy space warmed by the sun, nothing to do but lie down and look at the sky. All around him, all day long, the breeze swirled and pulled things together so that the cabin began to neaten: shoeboxes of bolts and screws and nails; picks and small shovels lined up in a corner; bait boxes and empty gasoline cans, scattered chunks of firewood, brushes and buckets and tubes of paint—all of it drawn together into tidy piles and rows.

His paintings became visible from new angles.

Every night he made a little mark in the wall with his thumbnail.

Every morning, waking to a miracle.

She was still too thin. Her nose was constantly dripping; her eyes were watery and red around their rims. She didn't eat much in the mornings or at night, only taking in the one big meal at midday. She liked potatoes and squash fried up with eggs, and soft-cooked beans mixed with brown sugar, and the hot dogs he'd bought at the Shell station and kept in the freezer. Apples and pears and peaches. She didn't eat the fried collards and onions he liked. She wouldn't stomach any lettuce. Often, after dark, he asked her to read aloud from his big Bible. If he felt up to it, he taught her the guitar. She was a fast learner, her long fingers able to manage the chords. He taught her the lyrics to Johnny Cash songs. He taught her to sing the healing song.

What surprised him was how matter-of-fact she sounded when she talked about what she'd done. How much money she'd made, and how the johns were rich and famous men—one of them even a judge—and how her manager gave her nice gifts. As far as the Prophet could tell that meant fast food and new clothes every now and then. He wanted to ask about her life before all of that. Did she have parents, sisters, brothers? Did she run away from home? He didn't want to scare her off. Watering sprouts with a hose would drown them. You had to wait till the roots took hold.

Then he reminded himself: she wouldn't take root. Couldn't. Not here. Time, times, and half a time, America about to witness the wages of what it had done. His own time running short, too. Against his will he was falling asleep more and more often, drifting off in the lower afternoons and waking in the slanted light of dusk. A hot spoke in his ribs tunneling a well, deep and wide.

He needed to tell her his plan and send her on her way.

But then he remembered his beautiful idea.

Two weeks since the rescue. It was raining. A nice steady soaking, the kind of rain he used to love for his crops. The cabin smelled musty. The roof leaked. He'd been meaning to tar up the gaps—another thing he'd forgotten to do since the girl came.

She'd brought a pile of washed towels and clothes in out of the rain and was draping them over lawn chairs by the woodstove. The Prophet lowered himself into his recliner, noticing, on the headrest, an oval of grease from his hair.

You been to school a lot, haven't you, Michael? he said. The girl had been showing him his spelling mistakes, such as where he wrote *gost* instead of *ghost*, *pryer* instead of *prayer*.

I guess so, she said.

I need your help with something, he said.

He opened his Bible. In the Old Testament there was always an announcement at the start of the prophets. Who the prophet was, and when he lived, who the main ruler was and what the visions were going to be about. He wanted something like that. An announcement board to hang above his front door. The board would be a kind of opening sentence, the vision paintings inside the cabin like chapters. His beautiful idea: the cabin would be a book people could walk around inside of.

He found a passage and asked Michael to read it aloud. She sat beside him and read in her confident way, only sounding out *Uzziah* and *Hezekiah*.

I want to paint something like that, he said when she finished. An announcement telling about me. The Watchman. My times and seasons.

The girl was looking at him with squinty eyes.

You're gray, she said. I mean your skin is—

Days of Clinton, Bush, and Obama, he said. Word of the Lord concerning Tennessee and Alabama and Georgia. And America. Hanging above the door like an opening sentence, see?

He handed her a pencil and notepad. She began to write, erased, started over.

Make some of them words uppercase, he said.

Stop watching, she said.

He lay back on the recliner and listened to her pencil scratching and grew impatient. Finally he stood and looked over her shoulder, then snatched the notebook from her so he could sound out what she'd written:

THE WORD OF THE LORD THAT CAME TO WATCHMAN OF LOOKOUT MOUNTAIN IN THE DAYS OF CLINTON BUSH AND OBAMA WHICH HE SAW CONCERNING ALABAMA GEORGIA

Words like in the Bible, but about him! He tried to read them aloud but a bulge blocked up his throat. The girl's looping letters twirled over the page. He swallowed to force the bulge down.

And also concerning America, he said. And the whole planet Earth. We got to add that.

She took the notebook from him and wrote.

I can write it big, she said. Paint it, too, if you want.

When He Saw His First Vision

1964

By the time he was sixteen years old, the Prophet—still known as Winston back then—was working on the bucket line at the Wheland Foundry. Men wearing goggles and thick gloves tipping molten iron out of giant urns suspended from hooks. The hot liquid poured like syrup into valve molds, which sat on trolleys that rolled along the tracks beneath. His first week on the line a new man tipped the bucket too fast, not respecting the gradual angle you had to create. Molten liquid leapt out of the mold like milk poured against the side of a tin cup. He had to plug his ears and hum the national anthem to drown out the man's screams. Fire licked outward, making slow work through the layers of human skin. Molten metal ate fast, straight down to the bone and right through. There was no recovering from it.

Now he was twenty-one and welding with the other Smiths and Johnsons. Draft dodger names. Most had registered as conscientious objectors. He'd learned to weld on his father's old oxyacetylene rig, the kind with two separate hoses, acetylene and oxygen, and brass couplings that had to be tightened constantly. When the supervisor found out he knew the basics, they moved him over to the fabrication shop and taught him to use the arc welder. Skilled workers were paid more than the men on the line. Only drawback was the heavy gear: helmet with its stifling visor, leather jacket, boots, cumbersome suede gloves. Unbearably hot in the summertime.

On the line he'd made brake castings and drums, cast-iron fittings and hydrants. Here, all they were doing was closing pipe joints. Quota was four joints an hour. He could have worked faster with CO_2, which gave a cleaner seam, but either way he liked chipping away the dark slag to reveal the silver beneath. He didn't know what the pipes were for. Probably Vietnam. The foundry had produced gun turrets for the navy in the last war, the one his father fought in.

One Friday night he clocked out early. Mid-October, still hot, his shared bedroom in the bunkhouse thick with humidity. He and some of the other workers were trying to get to the drag races in Fort Oglethorpe. They waited near an hour for their ride to show, and when the ride didn't come, they decided to hitchhike across the river. A tent revival meeting was there, the men told him, with a fake preacher working fake healings.

He'd heard about these kinds of meetings and intended never to set foot in one. Now here he was, watching a preacher pace back and forth across the stage with a choir swaying behind him. When the preacher flung his arms out over the crowd, a hot wave pushed him backward and he found himself looking up at a clover-shaped stain on the tarp. A woman's face appeared above him. God bless you, brother, she said, handing him a small Bible, a nice one, with gold-edged pages and little finger tabs for the chapters.

He took the Bible home and shoved it beneath his cot. From time to time he thought of it under there, like a thick block of money with stairsteps cut into the gold. People who read the Bible thought the answer to things getting better was in another world. They trusted in a God who was supposed to be three in one and one in three. But the only trinity he knew of was the one the men in the foundry talked about: Government plus Big Business plus Church. Three joined together as one to keep the working class down.

That night he couldn't sleep. He kept thinking about the falling backward and the three-leaf clover shape on the canvas tent. He pulled out the Bible and tried to read some pages in the front, but for the most part he couldn't understand a word. The red words in back were easier. The things Jesus said. His aunt used to drag him along to Sunday school so he'd seen pictures of the man in white robes with children at his feet, the near-naked body drooping on the cross, and the dead body draped across a woman's lap. In the pictures Jesus had seemed like a pushover who would just take it from people. Red-words Jesus was different. Red-words Jesus had a whip and a temper. He told people off and didn't give a damn. A crowd tried to push him off a cliff and he walked right through them.

The next day, when the noon whistle blew, Winston set his helmet and goggles on the shelf and hung his coat and gloves on the hooks beneath. He waited in the lunch-pail line, but instead of eating in the room beside the infirmary with the other welders, he went down to the foundry floor. Here, the men climbed ladders and ate their lunches sitting up in the high windowsills. The foundry smelled like blood, grease, and sweat mixed together, but up on the sills you could taste your food. Sometimes you could catch a breeze carrying the scent of leather from the tannery and the smell of ribs at Hattie's Bar-b-que. From one corner, if you twisted your neck right, you could see Chattanooga Creek.

He spotted his friend Clarence in his usual spot, legs dangling, face shining with sweat. Winston climbed up to sit beside him.

There he is, Clarence said.

How's it going? he asked Clarence, opening his pail.

Same's it always goes, Clarence said.

I got a question: you ever seen a preacher make someone fall?

Sure I have.

That kind of thing ever happen in the Bible?

You done fell, didn't you, Clarence said.

Not saying I did and not saying I didn't, he said.

Winston laid out his lunch. Two chicken wings, sliced ham wrapped in wax paper, two hard-boiled eggs, a green apple. Flask of whiskey in his pocket. He always offered Clarence a swig. No, sir, Clarence always said, I got three kids at home and a fourth on the way.

Hey, Clarence said. Some of us taking the bus to Lovell Field later. President's coming here to make a speech about the war and civil rights.

What president? he said.

Ours, Clarence said.

I don't put no stock in politicians, he said. And I got plans to see a lady tonight.

Christ Almighty, Clarence said.

Christ got nothing to do with her, he said.

President Johnson. Why would anyone waste their time listening to a politician talk about civil rights? Politicians were the ones at fault, setting the whites against the Blacks so they wouldn't join together to fight the real enemy: the Unholy American Trinity. Businesses taking the sweat of the poor and turning it into fancy cars and airplanes; government taking money from their paychecks to make rich neighborhoods prettier and show the world how America is better than other countries; preachers humiliating them for enjoying God-given pleasures, food and drink and women. The lady he visited at the brothel. And as long as there was a race problem, the government gained power, businesses got richer, and preachers fattened themselves and their churches.

When the whistle blew he put up his pail and got into his helmet and gloves and jacket. Four joints an hour, fifty cents a joint. And if you welded just one joint wrong, you'd have burst dams, you'd have sewage on the streets and broken-down bridges. Doctors made a fortune to keep the human machine running. And here they were, at the U.S. Pipe and Wheland Foundry, keeping the machine called America running and making next to nothing doing it. Workers pouring the backbone and limbs, welders shaping the skeleton, sealing together the bones of a nation. And who were the doctors and lawyers, the politicians and bankers? The soft tissue sitting overtop. Flesh thinking it was independent of the bones underneath, detaching itself and starting to dry up. And the rotting lips kept making speeches at airports. Madness. America was consuming itself. A snake with its tail in its mouth.

He flipped down his visor—the familiar feeling of dropping beneath the ocean. He positioned the rod, pulled the trigger, and watched the little sun begin to form. Lit stars jumped out from the center of the arc. He liked this part, the careful weave back and forth across the line, the hot metal pooling. Like forming a galaxy. In the middle of the slag, the sun expanded. Too much heat. He took his finger off the trigger, then shut down the machine. Still the bright white ball grew, expanding until it was like a movie theater screen in front of him.

Clean-sheet white, five feet square.

On the screen was a bridge like the one down-town, rust-colored scaffolding above a string of wooden planks. There were people on the bridge—hundreds of them—all walking in the same direction. Some wore suits and walked quickly like they had to get somewhere. Some rode bikes. Some were pushing babies in strollers. Roller skates, wheelchairs, skateboards. A mother and father pulled a baby in a wagon. He looked ahead to see where everyone was going. But the bridge ended before it reached the other side. One by one the people reached the edge of the bridge and stepped off.

Hang on, he said, the bridge ain't finished, work-ers must've quit before it was done—but now he was on the bridge. To his left, a girl pedaled a bicycle with purple ribbons threaded into the wheels. To his right, a man carried a toddler on his shoulders. In front of him, a teenage couple had stopped to kiss.

Looka here, he said to the teenagers, we need to go the other way.

Stop, he said to the girl on the bicycle. You gotta go back!

No one seemed to hear. He turned around and only then did he feel the invisible wave shoving against him. As long as he moved in the same direction as the wave, he didn't know it was there. It was only in going against it that he felt its strength. The closer he got to the bridge's ragged edge, the harder the wave pushed and the faster the people around him moved. One by one bodies fell in silence. They put up no resistance. Just another step, and then *poof*. Gone.

He'd reached the edge. What was down there? A river, a valley, molten metal? His vision was blurred. The visor, he needed to lift it to get a better view . . .

He flung off his helmet; it rattled on the concrete floor. The joint had split clean in half. Another one like that and he'd lose his job. Goddamn whiskey. He was skunked. He needed to take a lesson from Clarence.

The man beside him had his visor up.

You're quitting? the man said.

Never said I was, Winston said.

You said someone quit before he finished.

I'd quit if I could, he said.

That goes for all of us, the man said.

After dinner he changed out of his work clothes into a button-down shirt and a clean pair of jeans, and when it was dusk he walked down Broad Street, cut over to Market, and continued on toward the river. By the time he reached the triangle-shaped building at the corner of King Street, his good shirt was soaked in sweat.

Downstairs, the Ellis Hotel was a restaurant and bar; upstairs was where his lady worked. He ordered a single shot of Jack and put it down quickly, then paid his tab, adding in the usual amount. The bartender handed him a key. Up the back stairs and down a corridor to the row of locked doors with heavy curtains hung just inside.

Her name was Margot. He'd been coming to see her for almost a year. He liked how she kept her hair piled up, with little strands loose around her face, and how she never wore lipstick. When he'd got himself undressed and was lying on the mattress, Margot removed her clothes in front of him, unhooking her brassiere last of all. Her breasts fell out heavily. She lifted one and then the other, wiping beneath them with a small towel.

He tugged on himself a little.

Let me, she said.

Don't know what's wrong tonight, he said after a few minutes.

Margot straddled his hips and leaned over to whisper into his ear. *Winston.* That was all it took. Just his name.

He got back after midnight. Normally on Ellis Hotel nights he fell asleep soon as he was on his cot. Tonight he lay awake. First time in his life he'd needed help in that kind of way. Even when Margot had him inside her and was moving, he'd kept picturing the man with the toddler on his shoulders, and the girl with the ribbons in her bicycle spokes, and how the wave couldn't be felt until you tried to go against it.

He had to get those pictures out of his head.

When the sky began to lighten he put on his shoes, slid the Bible from beneath his cot and went over to the common room. Beside the pay phone was a cup of pencils. He chose one with a nice sharp tip and good eraser, then sat on the hard-backed couch. There were some blank white pages in the front of the Bible, and some in the back, after a set of old maps. He took up the pencil and—though he'd never drawn a thing in his life—began to sketch the bridge.

Lost Eden

2014

Michael was sitting on the floor, writing on torn bits of masking tape: *Quincy*, *Black Coco*, *King of the Garden*, *Red Hawk*. Pink pintos and black turtles, pale limas and wine-colored kidneys. Last summer he'd picked the pods and plucked out the bean seeds by hand, spreading them on blankets in the sun. By the time they'd dried he was tired just looking at them. He dumped them into a barrel, tens of thousands of beans, the four varieties all mixed together. He figured he'd get around to sorting them. Now she was doing it for him.

The Prophet had started to draw some jugs on the ceiling, but after a few minutes he gave up and lay back in his recliner. His ankles and feet were puffy and yellowish. He didn't like the look of them. The girl had been here for over three weeks now. More and more often he forgot the reason he'd brought her. He forgot about telling her his plan. Sometimes he imagined that she'd always been here taking care of things.

He'd heard her go in and out the back door a few times last night. Well, it was hot out. Likely she was drinking more. It was somewhere in the middle of May; he wasn't sure of the date. He'd long ago stopped worrying about clock setting, the forward and the backward. Another mile farther into Alabama and the sun rose and set an hour sooner, which proved time was nothing, just a sheet of wax paper laid over everything you could see. But if you could get up above the wax, above the Earth and into space where you could see the planet—a bright spinning thing—you would see how time was nothing but a shifting in and out of sunlight.

All the time behind him and all the time in front of him: one long day.

He didn't put the TURN HERE 4 TOMATOS sign out this year. He wouldn't have much to sell. But the main reason was to cut down on visitors. Mae Thomas used to show up regular to check in on him, but she was old now, had to be near ninety. As a precaution he'd told Michael she should go out back if a visitor came. You never know when a lost tourist might show up, he said. Someone sees you here they might tell the police. The dark expression swiping her face. All the bad things been done to her. The way to get the bad things out of your head was to draw them. Over and over, you could empty your head by getting what you saw out on a piece of paper.

Today she had on athletic shorts and a T-shirt with a
stick figure holding a rainbow-striped apple. Macintosh.
She was humming the mulberry tree song. She had a
pretty voice. Nothing she could get famous for like Zeke.
But a nice clean sound, with quivers like afterthoughts
on the downsides of notes. He spat into his bucket and
took a few shallow breaths. Felt like dragging air up
through a straw. A new pain, triangle shaped, was lodged
up in his lower spine. He could stand the pain. It was
the breathing that worried him. The dizziness when he
stood, and the blood bubbles gurgling between his lips.
Was Zeke's number still programmed inside the phone?
Maybe Michael could show him how to use it. Lately
he'd been thinking Zeke might like to meet Michael.
Maybe he could tell the story of the rescue in such a way
as to make his son proud.

He'd had another thought, too. Every time this other
thought came up, he shoved it away. Now, listening to
the girl's voice, watching her stick the pieces of tape
across lids, the thought came again: she could have a
new family in Nashville. Be a big sister to Sullivan.

She took a stack of lids and some jars into the
kitchen annex. He heard the slosh of water. When she
came back she was holding a magazine.

You need dish soap, she said.

Need a lot of things, he said.

Can I show you something? she asked. Outside,
where it's good light?

Sure, he said. Help me up a minute.

The girl pulled him to standing. He leaned on her until he got his legs under him, and they went out to the front porch rockers. He'd planned to paint her name across the back of Zeke's rocker as a surprise, but when he'd seen her handwriting with its swirls, he asked her to write it in pencil herself, then painted over the letters in bright blue.

Michael handed him the open *National Geographic*. Lost Eden: Land of the Havasupai.

It's the Grand Canyon, she said. It's where I'm going to live someday.

Which state was the Grand Canyon? He couldn't remember.

You can see more stars than anywhere else on Earth, she said.

He took the magazine and turned some pages: the Milky Way above dark peaks, brown- and orange- and red-striped cliffs at sunset, coyotes against a desert background, and some animals that looked like deer but shorter, with fat horns. A man with poles walking on a dirt path above a river the color of grass. The cliff drop beside the man in the picture was so steep the Prophet felt quivery in the tops of his thighs.

No boats are allowed on the river, she said, except the kind you have to paddle yourself.

How're you gonna get food down in there? he said. Or go to school?

She showed him pictures of a village: a stone church with a red door, a windmill above waterfalls tumbling into turquoise pools. He had to admit the turquoise color was magnificent. And here were women in skirts working in a garden, growing vegetables. A garden in the desert! It was an image of the future foretold by the prophets: the myrtle instead of the briar, green trees instead of cactus, a dry land turned ripe.

This here garden, he said. This is what we're doing inside the cabin.

If you help me, she said, if you can give me the money—

We could fill the tree of life with fruit, he said. Paint vines over the entire ceiling!

Anyhow it's just an old magazine, she said.

She went inside. He looked at the date on the cover: 1964. He would have been twenty-one. Working at the foundry, steeping his lungs in the asbestos. A mistake to talk about painting the cabin when she showed him the lost Eden. Maybe now she'd leave. All this time he'd had—he'd been wasting it. Like the faithless servant who buried his one talent.

He closed his eyes and watched for the spinning circles. Nothing. His heart double-timed. He'd go back inside. Plenty of stars to see here in winter, he'd say. If you come back after you do the important job, you're welcome to live here long as you want.

What job? she'd say. Come back from where?

That's what I've been a-wanting to talk to you about, he'd say.

He stood and was about to go inside when he heard tires coming up the driveway. He didn't have to look to know who it was: somebody bringing Render Simms, the blind man with his bamboo navigating pole. He'd smelled his disease oil last night, or maybe dreamt he'd smelled it, a stink clinging to the clean particles bumping around in his cabin, sharp and salty like rotting fish.

He hurried inside and bolted the door.

Visitors, he said. He threw his blanket off his raft and leaned it up against the back wall. You need to go out back.

I feel sick, she said. Something I ate. Just leave the curtains closed, I won't—

He yanked aside the sheet.

Too risky, he said.

Silently, she went out the back door while he gathered up the lids with her handwriting and stashed them in a kitchen cupboard. Voices, the tap of Render's bamboo pole on the porch steps. The Prophet let himself have a good cough and wiped his mouth with his bandana. When he stepped outside the oil stink was so strong he had to pinch his own leg through his pants pocket to keep from gagging. There was another scent, too. Sweet like the vanilla cookies Zeke used to dunk in his milk.

Render's sister was bringing him today. Denise. Last time she'd come she left Render in the car and walked up to the door alone and—without even saying hello—told the Prophet she was tired of watching her brother suffer, tired of waking up every day wishing he were dead.

All these years you been giving him nothing but false hope, Denise said. If your singing wasn't such a comfort to him.

Render had on socks with sandals, drawstring shorts, and a button-up shirt printed with exotic-looking flowers. In the shade of the porch Denise removed her brother's sunglasses. Render's eyes looked everywhere and nowhere. His body quivered, one hand holding his pole, the other moving through the air like he was conducting some uncertain music.

The Prophet helped Denise get him inside. Denise had the diabetes, too, but it hadn't got hold of her the way it had her brother. The Prophet took shallow breaths. He didn't want Denise to hear the wheeze. From behind, Denise pushed on Render's kneecaps till the man's legs were bent enough to allow the Prophet to slide a chair beneath. Render sat clutching the pole the way a child might hold on to a rope swing.

I'll wait in the car, Denise said. Gimme a wave when you're done.

Render had on a military hat stuck with pins, mostly American flags. In the center, just above the brim, was the Purple Heart the government gave him. The Prophet couldn't remember what he'd done to earn it. He removed Render's hat, knelt in front of him, and put his hands on the man's shivering legs.

How you feeling today, brother?

Yooooouuuuu, Render said. Sooooouuuung.

Song won't work, the Prophet said. Smell's too strong, see?

Render's head moved in all ways—yes, no, I don't know. But the Prophet could tell by his eyes that he understood.

It's not just the smell, he said. I can't hardly draw breath enough myself.

Render's hand fluttered around until it came to rest on the top of the Prophet's head.

Your suffering ain't all bad, the Prophet said. I smell a sweetness, too. It's a suffering unto glory, what it is. You'll be in the garden of the Lord before you know it. Nothing to say but thank you all day long.

Spittle bubbled in the corners of Render's lips, his mouth opening and closing.

Sooooung, he said.

The Prophet went to the window and lifted the work shirt he'd hung up for a curtain: Denise was sitting the car, looking down at something.

He slid the front door bolt into place.

I want to introduce you to someone, he said to Render.

He found Michael sitting just outside the back door. He could smell that she'd been sick.

The eggs, she said. You need a fridge.

Come on in here and meet Render. He's no one to worry about; he can't see or talk.

What's wrong with him?

Parkinson's. Diabetes. Death smell's strong on him. He knows it.

Render's pole had fallen to the floor, and he was leaning over feeling around for it. Michael knelt to pick it up and Render reached out to touch her face and hair.

It's one of them comforting angels I told you about, the Prophet said.

Soooooung, Render said.

Did you sing it for him? Michael asked.

Won't do him any good, the Prophet said.

The song that came from the girl's mouth filled the cabin. She sang about the mulberry tree but changed the words so that instead of the sound moving through the tree, it was the tree itself making the music. That wasn't how it went in the Bible. The Prophet didn't mind. He didn't mind!

A low rumbling came from Render's chest and turned to a high-pitched tremble in his throat, coming out in a wail. The Prophet assumed the man was crying. But he saw that Render's lips were curling up, his eyes bright, and he wondered if some deep-inside part of Render—some part still untouched by the disease oil—was laughing. Maybe it was only his chest and throat muscles betraying him.

The girl stopped singing. The Prophet held Render's face steady until he was quiet.

See now, the Prophet said. You got your own song to sing.

Render fumbled in his shorts pocket, pulling out one fifty, and then another.

I can't take your money, the Prophet said.

But he was handing the bills to the girl. She folded them and put them in her pocket.

Thank you very much, she said.

A Time for Fighting and a Time for Holding Still
1943–1959

But before he was the Prophet, Winston was a regular devil like the rest.

Born in Mentone, Alabama, 1943. A sister named Caroline, three years older. His father shipped to France a week after he was born and came home a year later damaged in some invisible way. Kept his lips pressed tight together and a hand to his lower back when he sat and when he stood. Friday nights some men he'd known in the war drove to Mentone from Birmingham and Fort Payne to play cards for money. Only when the men came did his father take the bottle out of the paper bag he kept it in.

His father was a welder, with a mask painted like a skull. He showed his son how to suit up and set the dials, and taught him the best way to lay a bead: zigzag forward, pull back, forward again. When Winston was nine his father let him quit school. Together they spent

their days in the garage, fixing broken-down cars. Those
were good days, not speaking, just working side by side.

Then came the surgery—paid for by the government—
which fused something in his father's spine so he couldn't
bend over to see what he was doing anymore. The brown
bag started coming out in the mornings. Often his father
washed down the pain pills with whiskey; by noon he'd
be slumped in his lawn chair in the garage.

His mama went back to cleaning houses and working nights at the truck stop. The men stopped coming to
play cards. And finally the pressed-together lips opened:
Goddamn cunt whore I'll cut your goddamn throat. He
wouldn't have dreamed his daddy's mouth could shape
such sounds.

One morning, a few months after the filthy words
had started up, he found his sister and mama arguing
about something in the kitchen. His sister had a lit cigarette loose in her fingers.

He done it to you again, didn't he, Caroline said.

His mother's cheek was bruised; she had her bottom lip tucked inside her mouth but he could see it was
swollen.

He don't know what he's doing, when he does it,
his mama said. Put that out.

I'll kill him, Caroline said, looking all around the
kitchen like their father might be hiding in one of the
cupboards.

You listen to me, his mother said. Your daddy seen things in that war. Boys hunting for their own blown-off arms.

I don't care what he seen, his sister said.

That evening his mama brought home a black-and-white television and set it on the kitchen table. She ran the cord over to the wall and plugged it in, then turned the dial and found the show with the man and his silly wife in an apartment in New York City.

Not another hat, the man in the suit said.

Now just wait until you've seen it, the woman said.

The Giffords let us borrow it a few days, she said. Just something to keep your mind occupied. See how you like it. Everyone has them now.

His daddy was steeped in whiskey. His mama moved the television so it was right in front of him—*Now don't you think it's beautiful, don't you think it's worth just any amount of money*—and he could see what her face must have looked like as a girl, the shy naked red in her cheeks. Embarrassing. He turned away and heard his mama make an *uh-uh* sound.

His father's fist was like a hammer trying to nail her down. Winston stepped between them and took two hard cracks on his cheek before his father went out the door, taking the bottle with him.

Two days later, a hunter found his body at the foot of a cliff in DeSoto.

It was the war that killed him, his mama said. Your father came home already dead. Just took his body some years to figure it out.

His mama took him and Caroline to live with an aunt in middle Georgia—Fort Valley, peach and pecan country. And now he learned what he was really good at. He could scramble up the wide-footed ladders and pick as much as three people, even with the heavy bag hanging around his neck. He could tell in a single glance if a fruit was ready or if it needed more time, or if the insects or birds had punctured it so it was rotted out in the middle. He liked being up with the red and gold fuzz and the bees, the sweet smells and bright spots of light changing shapes on the ground when a breeze came through.

One day, when he was sixteen, he'd set a ladder on a yellow jacket nest and got a line of stings up his leg. He came down and poured water from the bucket on the welts. Goddamn white trash farmhand wasting the drinking water, Curtis said. Curtis was the super's son. He didn't care about the water; he was angry because of Caroline. Curtis had tried to court her but Caroline ran off with a picker named Oscar instead. Now they were two workers down and the rest of the workers had to make up the difference.

Since they'd come to live with the pickers, Winston had learned that you were at the bottom until you beat someone up. Then you moved into their place. It was the way to make things better for yourself if you didn't have money. He would only fight men who weren't drunk. Fighting someone drunk was worse than being a pussy.

You got to stop with the fighting, his mama said. They were in his aunt's trailer at the end of the day. July, harvest season, so many peaches this year he had to keep picking into the dark, feeling around in the branches.

Have to fight, he said. Curtis said Caroline whored herself.

Him saying it don't make it true, his mama said.

I ain't going to just take it, he said.

Jesus turned a cheek, his aunt said. It's the turning what makes you strong.

Goddamn Baptists. His aunt dragging him and his mama along with her every Sunday. Turn a cheek was what women and cowards said. That was the problem with the churchgoers and it was the problem with Jesus Christ himself. Taking it from everyone, getting himself nailed up dead.

He'd found a bowie knife in the garage after his father was buried. Doubled-edged and curled at the tip. His mama didn't know he had it. Next time Curtis said, Your sister given birth to her bastard baby yet? he'd have it under his belt. Not to use. Only to show as a threat.

He was in the top branches of an Elberta when Curtis knocked the ladder out from under him. He felt his chin split on a limb before he hit the ground. The thudding of the peaches, the perfect tip-top ones he'd set gently in his neck bag. He spit out a tooth and a piece of another. Between his ears, a sound like a wet finger rimming a glass. He reached for his waistband—where was the knife? There, on the ground—

No white trash gonna scare me with—

Curtis's cheek skin curled open like a petal. He could see the dark liquid rushing in to cover grayish bone. Curtis folded over himself, screaming.

They would kill him. They'd arrest him and he'd go to prison.

He started to run and felt himself lifted off his feet. *Don't make a sound.*

It was John-Early, another picker, one of Oscar's friends. John-Early slung him over his shoulder and ran away from the orchard, across the fallow fields toward the woods bordering the highway. Remember everything I'm about to tell you, John-Early said. Hitch a ride to Chattanooga. Place called Wheland Foundry on Broad Street. Ask for Clarence. Tell him I said to put you on the line. I'll tell your mama.

When they reached the tree line John-Early set him down, told him which direction to go, and put a handful of bills and a half-eaten stick of jerky in his hand.

There's a time for fighting and a time for holding still, John-Early said. You got to learn which is which.

Warfaring Angels Will Descend

2014

The Prophet had stayed out far too late. He couldn't remember where he'd been or who he'd been with. Now it was after midnight and he was walking home. A clear, moonless night, star-drenched. Honeysuckle and privet shimmered on either side of him. He turned onto his dirt road and walked through silver-lit woods until he reached his driveway.

His cabin was gone. In its place was the trailer where he lived with his mother and aunt. They'd be asleep. He didn't want to wake them.

He pushed open the screen. Smells of orange and vanilla and clove hung thick inside. Beautiful smells! When his eyes adjusted to the darkness he saw chocolate chip cookies, sugar cookies, ginger snaps; peach cobblers, pecan pies, cherry and apple tarts; cupcakes frosted every color and speckled with rainbow candies—all of it piled in a great triangular heap on the kitchen table. The single bulb hanging from the ceiling rested sideways on a birthday cake with lit candles wavering in the darkness.

He remembered. Today was his birthday. He'd forgotten to show up to his own party.

He sat and forked a bite of the pecan pie into his mouth, swallowing without chewing. A nut lodged in his throat. He tried to hack it out but couldn't draw a breath. He began to run in circles around the table, clutching at his neck. He lay on the linoleum and thrust his finger deep inside his throat, trying to hook his finger around the nut. The light bulb switched on. His aunt stood over him, wearing the Frisbee-shaped hat she favored for churchgoing.

Get up, she said, reaching down to shake his arm.

Get up get up get up—

He was on his raft. On the ceiling above him were the jugs he'd started yesterday, in his nostrils the taste of orange-scented pecan. He raised himself up on his elbows and opened his mouth to say, Good morning, Michael, but the coughing took him.

I'll get water, the girl said.

He covered his mouth and felt a warmth in his palm: a plug of blood and mucus, putrid and thick as spackle. He wrapped it in his bandana and stuffed it beneath the raft. Michael came back with a mug but only a bit of the water went down his throat. The rest spilled down his chin and chest and wet his blanket.

Morning, Michael, he managed to say.

Your lips were blue, she said.

Just some allergies caught up in my throat, he said.

Happy birthday, she said. Sorry it's burnt.

On a plate beside his mattress was a thick pancake with black edges and whitish glaze melting on top. Three lit candles, burnt almost to their ends.

How you know it's my birthday? he asked.

You said seventy-one May eighteenth. That's today. You don't have to eat it.

Truth was he didn't know his real birthday. He chose a different date every year. He took a bite and let it set on his tongue. Dry and crumbly, with an orange aftertaste so sweet he felt the saliva rush into the corners of his mouth. He wondered where she'd got the sugar. He didn't think he had any. He didn't have oranges, or anything orange flavored.

A jolt of fear sucked his stomach through the floor, taking the pain down with it so that he was able to draw a full breath. He threw off his blanket, adrenaline tingling in his forearms and fingertips.

Wait, the girl said. But he'd already seen the cake-mix box and the half-full tub of frosting.

Where'd you get them things, Michael?

I wanted it to be a surprise—

Where?

Shell station.

When did you go there? Which day?

Yesterday. After the blind man left. You were sleeping. It's such a short drive, I didn't think you'd mind if I—

He held on to the counter.

You done *drove* there?

Your van's easy. Jackson taught me on a stick.

You just walked on in and bought them things?

Took them. No one saw.

He was afraid he might let out a sob. Likely there were cameras. Wouldn't take long to put his van and the video footage together.

He began to gather up jars and cans and shove them back into the neatened cupboards. He hated the organized rows she'd made of his things. He wanted everything messy, the way it was before.

The visions, getting her to the White House. That was the important thing. He told this to his brain, but the feeling in his chest was telling him different.

The important thing was having this girl around.

He stumbled to the porch and let the coughing take him. This time it held on and wouldn't let go. He dropped to his hands and knees and tried to suck breaths between his lips, but whatever door was open between the air outside him and the apparatus inside him was nearly closed. Getting her through the withdrawal, making sure she had food and things to do, a safe place to get well. What did he care about America? Just some lines drawn on a map, a flag, some names and dates. You couldn't feel anything about them.

Here she was, her bare feet in front of him, she was handing him a damp towel. He wiped his face and his hands and swiped at the blood on the floorboards. He felt her lift under his armpits. She helped him get settled into his rocker.

She could've left anytime she wanted, then. Could've taken his keys and drove herself. She'd stayed. The Lord was keeping her here, waiting on him to tell her the plan. And he'd been putting it off, not telling. He was the unfaithful servant. He'd be cast into outer darkness.

Michael, he said. I got to tell you some things.

His heartbeat a thin quiver, too fast—

You should rest, the girl said.

There's a tank in the shed, he said. You seen it there, behind the rakes?

I think so, she said.

I need you to get it, he said. And a paper bag in the feed bin. You'll have to dig. Then come back and write down everything I tell you.

Once he was settled in his recliner with the cool air flowing up inside his nostrils, his heartbeat slowed to regular. He wished he would've asked the girl to bring up the tank before now. She gave him the three bottles of pills but he couldn't remember which did what, so she read him the instructions on the foldout papers. As far as he could make out, one kind of pill was for breathing, one for pain, and one for sleep. He took two of the ones for pain and two of the ones for breathing.

Two-Step was back in his place beside the woodstove. The Prophet might've smelled the smoke sooner if it wasn't for the tubes in his nose. The devil's knees were drawn up, arms wrapped around his shins, forehead bowed. No hat. The thin head appeared pale as an eggshell. *Go on and try to stop me now*, the Prophet thought, picturing the stage, the audience, himself making the giant X.

The girl was pushing buttons on the phone.

It's dead, she said. There's no charger. At least I couldn't find—

Washington, DC, he interrupted.

Her eyelids flew wide.

You know where that is, Michael?

Why? she said.

I'm sending you there, he said.

The girl's cheeks had turned bright pink; the rest of her face was pale.

I got bus money for you, and some extra for food and taxis. And you got that hundred from Render.

You are giving me money, she said.

To get to Washington, he said. You don't have to be scared.

The air was flowing easy, easy. And Two-Step not saying a word.

The Prophet ripped out some notebook pages and folded them in half, and then in half again, making a booklet. He made some crude sketches, then held the booklet out to show the girl.

In Washington is the important job I been telling you about, he said. Looka here. The donkeys. You know about them. The president bouncing on the planet, celebrating, that was the first election. Next donkey is the president two years ago. See how he's fat with bags of troubles. Number three is Big-Tears. That's him now.

The girl's eyes darted around the cabin, the old husk drawn up over her face.

He swallowed. Then, his hand shaking, he drew two humped shapes, and above them a rectangle filled with dots. He glanced over at Two-Step, motionless in his corner, naked head bowed. Why wasn't he trying to stop him?

These here are beehives, the Prophet said. Two future wars. First war'll be like the other big wars. Countries fighting against countries. Second war's gonna be different. Every army in the world combined, swarming up to outer space. We're gonna sting 'em to death, the bee soldiers will say. But it's warfaring angels coming down to fight an ancient evil hiding under the ocean. The president needs to get on the televisions, see, and on the internet systems. He needs to tell the soldiers to stand down; say to the people of the Earth, Do not be afraid, the Lord your God will fight for you. You only gotta be still.

Michael just stood with her mouth open. The Prophet
flipped through the sketches, adding details here and there.
At the bottom corner of the last page, for a signature, he
drew a stick figure of himself wearing Two-Step's hat. He
handed the booklet to the girl. He could see her crowded
bottom teeth. He noticed she had a mosquito bite on her
cheek, raised red with a white halo.

One more thing, he said. My son, Zeke. Nashville
would be a good place to come back to. You could be
like a sister to Sullivan.

You mean go there after Washington? she said.

The husk hiding whatever it was she wanted to say,
or was afraid of saying.

Listen, Michael, he said. You think you chose what
you done, but you're just a child, see? No matter what's
been done to you—

He meant to say, You are beloved, but couldn't get
the words out.

The breeze she made, the happiness.

Two-Step silent in his corner.

Take the phone, he said. Zeke put his number in
there. You'll find a charger somewhere.

Tomorrow, the girl said.

Tomorrow what?

Tomorrow I'll go to Washington, like you want
me to.

Son, His Only Son!
1964-2014

He sketched the unfinished bridge over and over on the blank Bible pages. When he ran out of space he bought himself a lined notebook and a set of colored pens. He liked doing the sketching more than anything else he'd done in his life so far. Fixing cars and picking fruit and welding pipes was taking what someone else made and changing it a little. Sketching was making something that never existed on the planet before.

He taped his bridge sketches beside his cot, where he could see them. He'd left white space at the bottom of each drawing. He didn't know what was down there, in the chasm.

Ten years passed before the screen dropped in on him again.

1974. By then he was thirty-one and living in Hinkles, out the back of Lookout Mountain. He and two other men from the foundry shared the rent on a trailer, three-bedroom. One of them had a used Chevrolet and did the driving up and down the mountain. The Prophet was making good money now, enough for food and rent and to chip in for gas, with plenty left over for whiskey and women. He couldn't say much was wrong with his life. But a kind of unease had settled over him. Like he'd forgotten to do something and couldn't remember what it was. He wondered if the unease had to do with Margot, his lady at the Ellis Hotel. Ex-lady. She'd moved to Chicago. Didn't even tell him she was going. One Friday he went upstairs and unlocked the door like always, but it was a skinny woman standing in front of the mirror, looking at herself.

He went out to find the matron. Where's Margot? he asked.

Gone home, she said. Agnes will take care of you.

He visited Agnes a few times. She never remembered his name.

And then came the day the visions returned. It was the middle of June. He'd taken off his coat and welding gloves and was standing at the urinal when the movie screen unscrolled in front of him. Clean-sheet white, five feet square. Hello! he said, surprised by how pleased he was to have the screen in front of him again. Hadn't had anything to drink, either. He zipped his fly and watched two feeble fried egg shapes merge together and pull apart. He waited to see if they'd turn into something he might recognize, but the screen rolled up and he was looking at the tiled wall.

He sketched the fried eggs quickly and hung the drawing above his stove, beside the drawing of the bridge.

Now the movie screen began to drop in regular. Most times it was just the floating fried eggs, merging together and pulling apart, like they were practicing. Once they came together into the shape of a woman draped over the side of a bed; another time they pulled apart into trees. While he watched the trees bent toward one another, slowly, twining up their branches to form an archway.

He bought acrylic paints and small brushes. Seemed like every time he finished a painting, the movie screen would drop down again.

That December, just before the holiday break, he got to work early and went to the front office. He planned to ask about his paycheck, how to adjust what the government was taking out of it. What he really wanted was to see the new woman from Soddy-Daisy who answered phones. He'd met her twice—once in the lunchroom, once in the parking lot. Both times, the way she'd looked at him made him feel shy, and somehow important.

He smoothed his hair before stepping inside.

She was at her desk, writing on a pad of yellow paper. He could see how neat her letters were, how evenly spaced. Her hair was long and straight and parted down the middle, the color of the tips of ripe cornstalks. She wore a dark-green blouse with a bow tied at the neck, and a pair of round, thick-rimmed glasses.

Morning, he said.

Hello, Winston, she said, taking off the glasses. She was looking at him funny. He glanced down to see if his shirt might be stained.

You mind if I ask you a question? she said.

Go ahead, he said.

Is it true you got the gift of seeing?

Who told you that? he asked.

Clarence, she said.

We go to the same church, she added in a way that sounded apologetic.

So: she was a Pentecostal. The dancing and moaning, the speaking in typewriter-click gibberish. She didn't seem the kind of woman to act that way, with her bow-tied blouse and tidy handwriting.

I guess Clarence got his own way of putting it, he said.

Well, I might be able to interpret, you ever want to show me your drawings.

They're paintings, he said. Started out with just drawing but now I'm laying on color.

She put her glasses on and went back to writing. Without looking up, she said:

Now you got an excuse to ask me out.

Six months later—June 1975—they were standing up at the courthouse. His bride wore a mint-green sundress and held a cluster of peonies she'd cut from a neighbor's yard. The buds were full of ants. While the judge spoke she pinched them off and flicked them gently to the floor.

She was twenty-four, the Prophet thirty-two. Together they had enough savings to buy a one-room trailer on a half acre of land out past Hinkles. The trailer had a screened porch attached, and a good-sized clearing the previous owner had left tilled and ready to plant. His wife quit the foundry and started working part-time at the Pentecostal church. The Prophet didn't attend any church. He wanted no part of organized religion and was grateful his wife didn't make a fuss about it.

Lord speaks to you a different kind of way, she said.

She'd been showing him how to interpret the visions. The unfinished bridge, she'd said, was people on the wide path that led to destruction. She showed him in his Bible where Christ talked about a chasm separating a rich man from a poor man named Lazarus, and said the chasm divided hell and heaven. People who tried to cross it without the blood of Christ were doomed.

You need to paint a cross over the chasm, she said, and show people walking on it to the other side.

Lucky, to have managed to find someone who didn't push him to change his ways. Never hid his alcohol or poured it out like the wives of some of his buddies.

His wife wanted him around the house more. She wanted a big family. Let's have us a full quiver, she said. When he asked her what that meant, she said she didn't know. It was just something people at church said when

---

a woman came up pregnant the third or fourth time: You'll soon have yourself a full quiver.

The Prophet left his job at the foundry in 1976. Seventeen years he'd worked there. Long enough. He went back to fixing cars and doing odd jobs around Hinkles, repairing radiators, laying tile. But it took four years to conceive the first, failed child, the one with the temple fuzz and the extra thumb.

Zeke came by way of scheduled C-section. The Prophet wasn't clear on the reason it had to be that way. Something about what they'd done to clean out his wife's insides.

1981. The Prophet was thirty-eight—an old age, he thought, to be having a first child. At the hospital he scrubbed his hands and wrists like the picture showed. Snapped on a shower cap made of thin paper, hooked a mask behind his ears, and followed a nurse through silver doors, down a hallway, and up to another door with a window. There was his wife's body, blue-draped, with a kind of curtain drawn up between her face and the rest of her. The Prophet thought of a magician he'd seen cut a woman in half.

Best not to look, the nurse said, leading him in.

His wife's mask was tucked beneath her chin so he could see her mouth was open. She had her eyebrows way up, like someone had just told her a secret, a nice one. A doctor and two nurses were already at work on her lower half.

Her arms were strapped down so he stood beside her head and put a hand on her shoulder. Now that he was here—the doctor talking about weekend plans, a nurse making a joke involving a birthday party at a steak house—he began to feel curious. He peered over the divider. He'd imagined a shallow reaching-in, the way he dipped his net beneath the surface to capture a fish, but the gray-green thing was already out and splayed across his wife's belly. The doctor seemed to be filleting with a kind of knife that burnt the flesh as it sliced.

The Prophet grasped the table.

You looked, didn't you, his wife said.

Couldn't see anything, he said. It was the only time he could remember lying to her.

He heard sucking sounds, the mew of a kitten. A wrinkled face covered in blood and white cheese curd floated up, slowly, above the curtain. The slits of its eyes were half-open and unblinking. The Prophet had the impression of an elderly religious figure, levitating.

When a nurse handed him a pair of scissors to cut the cord, he said, No, thank you.

Go on and cut it, his wife said.

Like slicing an earlobe, he'd say in later years, when he told the story of Zeke's birth.

His wife strapped the newborn into a little bouncy chair and moved him from place to place while she worked in the garden. Zeke rested one hand overtop of the other on his belly in a meditative posture. One windy day the Prophet noticed that each time a breeze crossed his son's face, Zeke squirmed and kicked and gulped for air but didn't cry. When the wind died down and he'd got his breath back, he went back to his formal watching posture.

He crawled at six months and walked at ten, holding on to a blown-up balloon like a steering wheel. At the age of two he wasn't saying any words or even making much in the way of sounds. His wife was concerned enough to call Mae Thomas. Mae looked in Zeke's ears. She snapped her fingers and made sounds from across the room. The child turned to look each time, unbothered. She took a flashlight and a Popsicle stick and probed around in his mouth.

He's tongue-tied's what he is, she said. Nothing to worry about. He'll talk when he's ready.

At the age of three his son began twisting up his lips and blinking his eyes while scratching sounds came from his throat and spittle bubbled at the corners of his mouth. Still no words the Prophet or his wife could identify. But two days after his fourth birthday Zeke began to speak in sentences. He formed words with air pockets in his cheeks. *Touch* and *church* began with tight-lipped twistings and ended in wet flapping jowls. The Prophet wondered if the boy had somehow known he'd have this impediment and had chosen to keep silent in order to delay the struggle.

Walker County put him in special-needs classes. The boy who never cried began to cry all day. After four months they decided to keep him home. Social workers came to visit, and his wife showed them the books she read to him, the math worksheets the schools sent home. They gave her some forms to sign, agreeing to administer standardized tests every so often. After that the county left them alone.

The Prophet played guitar and sang hymns in the evenings, and that's when Zeke began to sing along with him. No stuttering when he sang. Every note perfectly pitched. His voice was high and pure, louder than a child his size should be able to make.

With a voice like that he won't need school, the Prophet said.

School's done him no favors, his wife said.

She'd taken sick. Parts of her disappearing, one by one, year after year. Breasts, hair, lymph nodes. She wandered around the trailer, picking things up and setting them down again. The medicine was expensive and the Prophet had to take extra jobs around town: mowing lawns, painting houses, tying up broken mufflers. On weekends he worked the fields while Zeke stayed inside and kept his mama company. Read to her, sang. He made himself grilled cheese and canned soup.

One evening when Zeke was twelve the Prophet came inside to find the two of them in silence: Zeke reading a magazine, his wife sleeping on the couch. He stood there looking at them, listening to the flipping of magazine pages, his wife's steady light snoring. He felt himself on the outside of something. Like his son and wife had gotten into a room together, and he could see them in there but couldn't find the door.

His wife was shrunken now. It was the end. She wept constantly, lying in bed or sitting in the recliner, listening to end-times preachers on the radio: the anti-Christ and One World Currency, the great persecution, with no one allowed to buy or sell unless they had the mark of the beast. The rebuilding of the temple in Jerusalem, Mount Zion, and the abomination that causes desolation set up on the Holy of Holies. The battle of Armageddon. Finally the part with Jesus touching down, the angels and trumpets and rising-up of bodies from their graves.

The following week the Prophet took his son to the new aquarium on the Chattanooga Riverfront. Once inside, they rode the escalator to the top floor and, in the darkness, descended ramps with an exhibit that followed a single raindrop from the Appalachians all the way to the Gulf of Mexico. The central five-stories-tall tank was visible on every level. Inside swam bigmouthed fish, rays, catfish that looked like sharks. The display read: RIVER GIANTS.

When they reached the bottom level Zeke stood with his face against the aquarium glass.

ALLIGATOR GAR. GIANT PANGASIUS. ARAPAIMA. WHIP RAY.

Biggest fish in the world's in the Bible, the Prophet told him. Called Leviathan.

How big? Zeke asked.

You add up all them fish in the tank, the Prophet said, and it wouldn't even be the size of one of Leviathan's scales.

B-b-big as a house? Zeke said.

Big as this here whole building, the Prophet said. But it's what's hiding under the ocean that matters. What warfaring angels are going to come down to fight someday.

In the darkness it was hard to tell if Zeke was interested. The Prophet worried he'd gone too far.

That night Zeke brought the Prophet a drawing: an open-mouthed fish with spiky teeth poking its head up out of the waves. Stars were falling down into the fish's gaping mouth. Underneath the drawing, Zeke had written: *Levithan*.

You see this in your head? the Prophet asked.

Zeke nodded.

You want to paint it big, like the ones I done?

Yeah, he said.

The Prophet had a stack of old cupboard doors taken off their hinges. He'd found them in the junkyard, and had been meaning to replace the ones in the kitchen. He gave

Zeke a cupboard door and a pencil and some paints and
watched as his son drew the fish. Together they painted
the sky blue, and the waves blue, but when Zeke started to
use blue for the fish, the Prophet mixed up some black and
white so he could make it shark colored. The sharp teeth
Zeke painted black. The stars were yellow and orange and
green dots loosening down the cupboard. Magnificent, to
have his son here painting beside him!

Did you paint that? his wife asked him later. He'd
removed one of the cupboard doors and replaced it with
Zeke's.

Zeke done it, he said.

It's me, isn't it, she said. Every piece of me swallowed up by this disease.

That ain't it, the Prophet said, it's—

No, listen, it's beautiful, she said.

While she suffered the hours felt like weeks, but when it
was over and he was looking back on the years with his
wife—eighteen years—it seemed he'd only known her a
matter of days. The funeral was held at the Pentecostal
church and afterward people brought him casseroles and
cards. Some of the cards had money tucked inside. He tried
not to let himself think it, but every so often the words
would appear inside his head: *Now Zeke's just my own.*

Came the good years. The cabin, shed, outhouse
with the cracked porcelain toilet. Tree of life holding up
the crossbeams. A place men could be happy together.

Not much space inside, but what did that matter? It was women who needed space. Men only needed things to keep them busy.

Zeke's stutter fell away with the onset of facial hair. He practiced his guitar, sang hymns in the voice that brought in enough money so they didn't have to worry all winter. The glow-in-the-dark wheels behind the Prophet's eyes bright and spinning every time he looked.

Then the fight at the country club. Johnny Cash dead, the Nashville money Cadillac-ing his son away.

Son, my only son! he cried out.

You'd've killed him if he stayed, Two-Step hissed. *Same way you'll kill the girl, sending her to Washington.*

What day was it, what year? Hadn't Zeke just been born? No: there were the girl's curtains, with the roses; there were the jugs he'd started on the ceiling above him.

Hush now, the Prophet said to Two-Step feebly.

Heat washed the length of his body. He shuddered, thinking of a piece of paper lit on fire, smoldering, curling in on itself. His organs and bones burning, a hot wetness—

He smelled urine, and another smell.

You done pissed and shit yourself, Two-Step said. *Who's rescuing who?*

Grayish light. Dawn or dusk, he wasn't sure. The tubes in his nostrils no longer spilling out the coolness. He let the hose drop to the floor, feeling his chest skin pull up tight to his ribs each time he drew a breath.

There was light coming from behind the girl's curtains, the sound of flipping magazine pages.

Leaving tomorrow.

He wanted to paint. He wanted to sit in his porch rocker beside the girl and wait for winter, when the brushstroke of the Milky Way would slingshot itself over the trees. Michael, he wanted to say, forget about Washington. Stay here where it's safe.

Selfish! Two-Step was right. Stealing, driving without a license. She wasn't a criminal before. His rescuing—kidnapping—had turned her into one. Turned himself into a criminal, too.

A damn third-grade-educated fool.

He slept, woke, slept again.

Michael, he called out into the darkness. Michael! The sound he made was barely a whisper.

He rolled off the raft and felt his way toward the girl's bed, crawling across the floor. His hands found the curtains, the mattress. Blankets folded neatly at the foot. The darkened lamp was cold.

She was gone, then. The day had passed.

Already on her way.

He crawled back to his raft and let the darkness take him.

I'm here.

The girl's face in the dim light, her hair hanging loose.

Thought you'd done gone already, the Prophet said.
Tomorrow, remember? It's still tonight.
Michael—
What?
You'll come back.
Yes.
Promise me.
I promise.
Michael?
Yeah?
I don't want you to go.
I know.

Song of Songs

Thou seest we are not all alone unhappy;
This wide and universal theatre
Presents more woeful pageants than the scene
Wherein we play in.

—Shakespeare, *As You Like It*, Act 2, Scene 7

May 19, 2014

When I open my eyes the red petals are pink, which means sunlight is touching, which means any minute he'll say, Good morning, Michael. I can hear him out there coughing and spitting into his bucket. Some mornings there's blood on his pillow, but if I mention it he says, Reminder of Christ's blood spilled out for the ransom of many, and here you are, Michael, ransomed without even any money. Well maybe that's true, only now this problem makes me wonder if a person can be unransomed. All right then wonder, go on and wonder.

My blanket is on the ground beside the mattress, sticky behind my knees and inside my armpits, just hot hot hot all night in my T-shirt. Through the gap in the curtains I see him up on the ladder beside the tree of life, which is surprising because of how bad he was yesterday. Sometimes he surprises himself, and me, too. He's changed out of the shit-stink pants into loose khakis with a shoelace for a belt and a plain white T-shirt. His choppy scribbled hair is the color of wet cement, dark paint in the wrinkles on the back of his neck like a spiderweb tattoo. He's got towels draped over the ladder steps so his feet don't split and bleed.

I stick my head out between the sheets.

You should put the lids on, I say.

He looks at the buckets and then at me, licking the part of his top lip that gets stuck to the bottom, the blue of his eyes still bright even with yellow threads grown over.

Morning, Michael, he says. I got a little energy to finish them jugs.

On the ceiling are two tipped-over pitchers, with streams of water coming out to make a fountain splashing down onto planet Earth. CUP OF GODS RATH is written in Sharpie beneath.

I need to put in a *w*, he says. Looked it up after I done it.

It should be *cups*, I say. There's two.

That's not how it's wrote in the Bible, he says.

Pull on jeans and socks and step into the room. Put the lids on the buckets and take the scattered small brushes to the kitchen. One of my jobs is to clean his brushes and another is to make sure there's enough water in the barrel. Brush my teeth with the little Barbie toothbrush he got for the granddaughter who never visits. Don't know my own grandbaby, he told me. Zeke doesn't want her here, doesn't believe the visions are of the Lord, and likely he'll burn the paintings when I'm gone.

Above the sink is a clock made from hands screwed on to an upside-down frying pan, with lines painted where numbers should be. It's always 4:50. The battery used to work but the second hand only pushed against the other two, all night going *click-click-click* but in the morning it was still 4:50. If I ask what time it is he tells me what's next to do, time to eat or time to paint or time to go outside and weed or water or pick. I can tell the time by the sounds outside. Mornings when it's still dark there's a bird that says, Miss, ter, *teeeeee*. And when the sun comes up one that says, Take a *rain* check a *rain* check a *rain* check. The one I call the Jimmy bird says, Jimmyjimmyjimmy, jimmyjimmyjimmy, always in threes like the dog who used to be at the window when I got home from school, barking *Let-me-out let-me-out let-me-out* when no one was in the foster house but Jackson, who would lock his bedroom door behind us. You're better than the other fosters we've had, Jackson said, you're the prettiest. Touching the new places beneath my shirt, and showing me where to touch on him, with the dog now on the other side of the bedroom door, saying *Let-me-in let-me-in let-me-in.*

Then come hymns from the faraway steeple, the one at noon about the mighty fortress and the one at six about once being lost but now being found. The old man said both songs are about me, that I am safe in God's fortress since he found me. Cicadas in the late afternoons, crickets at dusk, and then the first part of darkness where the frogs clack like beads up in the trees. Sometimes, in the middle part of the night, coyotes like children on a playground, celebrating something. Then the section of quiet before the birds start again. Quiet except for his coughing and spitting.

I come back from the kitchen and see he's climbed down the ladder and taken his shirt off so I have to focus on not looking at the old-man skin with its dark bruised spots and black-beetle moles. His feet are caked with dirt so you can't see the toenails except for their yellow tips. Shoes hurt his feet because of the swelling, but he said packed dirt makes a built-in shoe. He said, Remember the famous artist whose feet grew into his boots while he was up on a ladder painting his visions? Never heard of him, I said. Well, I'm like him, he said. God gave me the feet of a hind on the mountains. Then he got out his big Bible with pages that smell like fire smoke and dirty hair and showed me where it says *As the deer panteth after the water.* And the parts about Hosea rescuing Gomer, and the Watchman of Israel, and flowers blooming in the desert. On his computer Jackson once showed me a picture of the Grand Canyon, a glass skywalk where you can look down at the desert between your feet and feel the place between your thighs that goes soft, like when I heard those men say *From her mother, left it on the counter, best not to read.*

I go behind the curtains and put on my denim jacket. In one pocket is the booklet of visions and the folded-up money held with a rubber band. In the other pocket is my list of steps. I will need more money and I know where to get it. First I'll have to get down the mountain. That is step number three. After that come five more steps. On step number eight, my problem will be over. I don't know what step number nine will be.

Between coughs he's humming the song about Lucifer and the tricks of six sixty-six: From his hands it came down, and from his sides and feet. Always something about blood. Soon he'll be back to sleep and when he wakes again he'll know I'm on the way. Thinking I'm doing what he said. I thought lying to him would be easy but I have to force myself not to think about it. Treating me nicer than anyone. Never let me touch him that way even though I tried at first, never let me do what Jessamine said I'm good at. King's been doing it with me for a long time, Jessamine said, and now he wants to do it with you, and if you do this for him he'll take care of you, don't you want to be taken care of and have nice things and keep living in the house and seeing Jackson, don't you want that, Michael? And me saying, Sure I want those things, sure I do.

Here there are no alarms, no one saying time for the car and the three-hour drive to the *Delta Queen*, the old riverboat in Chattanooga they turned into a hotel—anchored now, not going anywhere, just sitting there rotting on the river alongside the park. The *Delta Queen* is where I met the rich johns from Backpage:

Sandpaper-man, who only wanted to watch me dance and rub me with his rough hands; Oldy-man, with the bald spot and strap-ons in a Whole Foods bag, who paid the most because of what he did, what King said I had to do for that much money; and Panda-man, the famous judge, the one who liked me in the blond wig. Michael—is that your real name—Michael never show me your real hair, Panda-man said, if I see your real hair I will kill myself, my own daughter is older than you. Panda-man is the one who gave me the fuzzy pouch shaped like a panda bear. Our secret, he said, ours and no one else's, I will put in extra cash just for you, see the zipper how it's hidden where the fur is thick? I will put money there every time and we'll keep it hidden on this boat. I know a good spot where they keep the old life jackets that no one even remembers, only don't tell your manager because they know who I am. Could lose everything. Family, career, reputation. Michael, here . . . I'm going to—right here—you want to feel good, don't you, angel? God. My angel.

Oldy-man was the worst but I liked how he dripped the sweet-smelling oil onto the vape cotton and put the cap on and let me inhale until my mouth and throat were prickly with butterscotch; liked to watch him inhale long and then put his open mouth just above the marble coffee table to exhale a little lake of fog. *Flick, flick* his hand would go, each flick twisting a funnel up out of the fog.

Tiny tornados in an upside-down storm. If my hands and legs were shaking, he'd give me more to drink and tell me I could sleep a little before we did what Backpage said. When Jessamine first told me about the drive to the rich johns—when she told me about Oldy-man and the strap-ons in the Whole Foods bag—I said, No way will I let anyone do that, no fucking way. Tried to jump out of the car, tore the dress, and even peed myself on purpose. So then the zip ties around my wrists and ankles, stopping at the gas station just before. To make sure I was looking like what the rich johns wanted. To give me enough pills to not have to feel it all the way. Every day they gave me the nice floating pills. Two, three a day. So when the alarm went off saying time for the boat I would be like Yes yes take me there please. But still the ties in the car, just in case.

Here no alarms no alcohol no smoking, only the smell of paint and gasoline and burning wood. Outside, the open field with a potato patch and a few rows of bent-over cornstalks, and beyond that the dark forest with the chicken shed in a clear sunny place. The day and night sounds telling the time. Always his coughing and spitting. Sometimes he stays awake long enough to play the guitar with the lamp lit and the stove popping a nice warm glow, and I think, *If only I could tell him my problem.* Tell him what else I stole from the Shell station. What I had to steal, to find out if I had two lines or one, yes or no. And so what if I wanted the cake mix, too, so what? To bake someone a cake on their birthday. Nicer than anyone.

I have imagined telling him the problem and the steps I need to do to fix it. Imagined him saying, That's okay, Michael, you will not be unransomed. But he wouldn't say that. Would never say it. And so I can't tell him the problem or steps.

He knows the first three steps. Step number one: cut off hair. He said I should make myself look different because even though it's been almost a month, the police or King, probably both, will still be looking for me. But let me tell you step number four, I imagine saying. Let me tell you step eight. And if he would make his signature on the consent papers, I would only have to go as far as Nashville. But surprise, he is sending me to Washington, DC, the closest place where no signature is required. Giving me the money to get there.

His shadow appears on the curtain.

Never done a flower like this one, he says. Come see.

His jaw's moving around like he's tasting something in there. His cheeks so sunk there's the outline of his gums and the hollow place on the side where he doesn't have teeth. His eyes go up and down, looking at me in my denim jacket. No more oxygen in his tank so his breathing goes *wheeee*.

Today's the day, then, he says.

It looks like a mustache, I say.

The flower he's painted is pink and split open into halves that swirl inward at their tips. Thick globs of red and white cover the stem.

Had a showing just now, he says. Curtains was covering the vision but I pulled them open, like this, and behind the curtains was two people climbing a hill. It was me and you, Michael. The devil was behind us throwing rocks but we kept on a-going, and when we come to the top, here was this flower. Hand me that yellow.

The yellow is almost empty. I can get you more paint, I told him once, I'm good at taking things without anyone knowing. But he said how could I think of stealing when I've been stolen so many times myself? Where'd you get all this paint? I asked. He said that when he gives away a painting and tells the interpretation, as a thank-you he asks the person to bring more paint. And they bring buckets of half-used house colors and bottles of school paints and tubes of acrylics. Trays and trays of watercolors. Once someone brought him a box of fat oil crayons, he said. Expensive.

With a brush he traces a bright yellow line around the mustache flower, holding up his shaking arm with the other hand. Twenty, thirty minutes is all he can stay awake before he goes back to bed. I told him he should paint on boards on the ground and nail them up on the ceiling when he's finished. He said that was the smartest thing anyone ever told him. Michael, you are smart, he

said, don't let anyone ever tell you different. There's a
test to get a diploma, I told him. And if I take it I can find
out what I'm good at, maybe social studies or reading,
which were my favorite subjects before. Or I'll find out
I'm not good at any of those things, only how to make
rich men in suits think they're on a date with a girl who
is at least eighteen.

Hand me a knife so I can press out some leaves,
he says.

On the shelf around the tree of life is a clean smooth
butter knife. I feel the metal in my hand and see my
reflection in the blade, stretched out cold like ice water,
like that time Oldy-man said, I'm not going to use this
but you need to hold still, hold still like I say. But the
one he took out of the Whole Foods bag was bigger than
usual and when he pushed I could feel it tear, and then I
was above myself seeing the girl on the bed with her face
pushed into the mattress and Oldy-man's white ass pocked
and sagging over the black straps, his skull like a shiny
kneecap poking up through his hair—holding the knife to
the side of the girl's neck, the feeling of cold water pouring out—but from up here she can see the knife is only a
toy, a child's pocketknife, and if she was strong enough
she would push him away. But no one chose this life for
her—she chose it herself, didn't she?—and then she's floating up higher, up above the boat's smokestack with the
gold *DQ* and the eagle clawing the swoosh of American
flag, the big red paddle and lights from the Market Street

Bridge shivering underwater, hearing the music as cars go across the bridge, three notes, high-low-high, *ahhhh-ohhhh-ahhhh*, the notes mixing with the sounds the girl on the bed is making. Then King kicking in the door, pulling Oldy-man off and hitting him in the face and stomach and crotch; Jessamine there, too, with her phone making camera noises. You motherfucker you didn't pay for that shit don't you ever do that to her again without paying or your wife and daughters will see your faggot ass see what you've been doing to my baby.

I bring the old man the butter knife but now he's sitting on his raft. Glitter in his hair and on his shoulders and his back where the skin pulls against his bones, a tight-squeezing sound rising like a question, *Wheee?*

Got a crick in my neck, he says. He leans over and lets his head rest on the part that blows up separate to make a pillow.

Let me get your pills, I say.

A privilege to suffer like Christ, he says.

Who made Christ suffer? I ask. I always ask and he always answers the same.

Made his own self suffer, he says. Devil thinks he done it, but it was God pulling the devil's strings.

He reaches out to touch my sneaker.

You're all set, then, Michael?

Yeah.

You got the taxi and bus money and them sample visions?

I show him the bills rolled up with a green rubber band and the little folded booklet.

You remember where to park?

Incline Railway, I say. In a visitor's spot.

Mae's grandson, he says. Jeremy. Tell him I sent you and he'll make sure you get down. Taxi to the Greyhound. Get on the right bus and all you got to do is stay on.

His eyes close. He told me that Jesus suffered and let himself get killed to save people from having to suffer. But the suffering never changed, not one thing changed. And how could the old man know that, tucked away out here in the woods, never going anywhere? He knows about the sickness kind of suffering, and the loneliness kind, but not about how if a john wasn't happy King had to punish me but left his hand open so I would get the peaceful feeling, like Yes, yes, I want to do everything you tell me. Please, thank you, yes.

Jessamine said it meant he loved me, that King hit with his hand open and gave me Wendy's or KFC after. No one was allowed to call him King but me. Other girls had to say Daddy. But I was King's favorite. My mother told me that when I was born the man who was my daddy came to the hospital and gave her a white flower even though he didn't want her to keep me and left her, after. *A lot of things I've done wrong but didn't get rid of you*, she said to me once. *No one could make me get rid of my own baby inside me.*

Light the fire in the woodstove, slice three potatoes and put them in the heavy frying pan with Crisco. Behind the stove, painted on the wall, are words from the Bible I helped him write. I AM GOD AND THERE IS NONE LIKE ME, FOR I WILL WORK A WORK IN YOUR DAY WHICH YOU WILL NOT BELIEVE THOUGH IT BE TOLD YOU. HABBAKUK.

He's got his work shirt hung over the window for a curtain so the light turns his skin purplish blue. His breath like scratching wind in pine trees. The yellow pills are for sleep, blue ones for pain, pink ones for breathing. I get three of the blue and three of the yellow, then stand over him with a jar of water. I could pour the water out onto his feet. How many jars would it take to get the mud off down to the skin?

With the tip of my sneaker I nudge his shoulder.

Hey, I say. Hey. You need to take your medicine.

Word of God's my medicine, he says in barely a whisper. Word of God and the healing song.

If I sing it, will you take the pills?

S'pose I will, he says.

He swallows all the pills without even opening his eyes while I sing the words about the mulberry tree and the sound of a-going that he told me is the story of God's army moving through the treetops. I sing until his jaw hangs loose and his breathing gets slow and quiet. David had to be still and listen before he went out to fight, he told me. Had to wait till he heard the sound in the trees because it meant God would go ahead of him. Sometimes the Lord makes us wait, he said, and if we're waiting, we better be listening, too.

The potatoes over there making a crisping sound. He loves potatoes more than any other food. Looka here, he said, look how hard and dry this one is, she's a ripe old grandmother but she keeps shooting out daughters.

I take two towels off the ladder steps and drape one over his chest, the other over his feet.

And now my heart is going fast because it's time to start the steps.

You'll come back then won't you Michael. Promise me. Could live with Zeke's family in Nashville.

But don't look at him or think about him now.

I pour some of his blue and yellow pills into a baggie and put that in my backpack. Stuff in my old dress and some underwear and socks and a roll of toilet paper. Also the phone, which even if I find a charger I won't use because maybe someone could track it. Anyhow there's no one whose number I know besides King's and Jackson's. But I will never call Jackson, never again because of when he stopped bringing me to his room. I do what I do for obvious reasons, Jackson said, you think I could afford that car on my own? You think it's love, but you'll learn, he said, the screen door going *snap-snap* behind him. Only three years older than me and not even a real foster brother. Hired by King to fake that he loved me and make me feel it back. But the phone is something I could sell.

Gather my hair into a ponytail and slice it off. Throw the hair into the stove and go all over with the scissors, a little bit at a time until it's gone and my hand rubs across my head to feel how short. Throw the instructions and wrapping into the fire, and the plastic stick with two lines saying Yes, yes, your problem is yes.

Step number one is done. One pocket with the visions and list of steps. The other pocket with a twenty for the taxi plus a hundred and ten for the bus ticket and the extra hundred from the blind man.

I slide half the browned potatoes onto a plate and wrap up the other half in foil. Put the wrapped potatoes in my backpack along with two hard-boiled eggs and the sad Barbie toothbrush. At least now he won't have to see it there beside the sink. I set the potatoes and fork on the floor beside him and watch until I see his chest moving. Toe his shoulder a couple times with my sneaker, to make sure he won't wake up. Put my hand on his neck to feel his heartbeat.

So quiet inside now with the potatoes done. Outside, the rasp of cicadas and the far-off sound of a mower or maybe a leaf blower. And here above his raft is the tipped-over whiskey bottle fastened to the wall, the green lizard coming out of the spout, PLAGUE IN DOGWOOD SEASON written above its head and I TOLD YOU SO on the long tongue. Piled in one corner are the saw blades painted like wide-open eyes.

You should hang them, I told him once. Attach the motor. Who cares if it's only eleven?

One less than twelve is bad, he said. One less is the devil's territory.

And in the kitchen the frying pan clock saying 4:50.

On a ripped-off flap of cardboard box I write with a Sharpie: *Thank you for helping me I will miss you love Michael. PS: I promise to come back.* One more egg and three slices of bread go into my backpack. Fill a sock with peanuts and tie it off and that goes in, too. And now there's nothing left but to take his keys and hat and sunglasses, get into his van, and drive to the Incline Railway.

Which is step number two.

How the day shines. All the tucked-away houses and trailers, churches coming one after another, cemeteries with fake flowers bunching up red, white, and blue. Every so often, around certain bends, the college that looks like a castle on the hill flings itself against the sky— look!—and disappears again. The old man said there was a professor there who once brought his students to see his paintings and who might put him in a book about the end-times and apocalypse. Someday, Michael, you will go to college, he said. Like my mother said she wished she would have done before the boyfriends started coming and going. Before doing what she did to herself. *Left a note on the counter, best not to read.* Three state shelters before the foster home in Macon, where the dog said *let-me-in* while Jackson and me were in his bedroom with the shadows of trees outside moving on the wallpaper. The foster parents going along, pretending not to know. Everyone paid by King—

No. Only think about now. I am on step number two, Drive to Incline Railway. Almost to step number three: Ride Incline train down mountain. The old man said he'd planned to drive me to the Greyhound himself, but just staying awake became a struggle. And me surprising him, already knowing how to drive, only needing to remember to keep the other foot off.

I can drive myself to the station, I said. But then realized he would not get his van back.

There's another way to get you down, Michael, he said. A more secret way.

I remember to slow down where the elementary school sits beside the pond with a red canoe tied to the dock. His crushed hat is sitting there on the dashboard and I put it on because city hall comes next. The most dangerous part of the drive, he said. Police keep a close watch for Fairyland stickers on bumpers, little badges to let them know who's local and who's a tourist. He doesn't have a sticker but he said the police know the look of his van. Just to be safe, when I pass the station I'm supposed to pull his hat low so it looks like him driving. But today is my lucky day, only one police car parked in front and no one inside it.

After city hall comes a stretch of big houses before the four-way stop at the border of Georgia and Tennessee. I look for the sign shaped like a train engine: WELCOME TO THE SCENIC CITY! Which means I am out of Alabama, out of Georgia.

Pass the Corner Café, the post office, the baseball diamond. Turn at the fountain beside the house with an American flag strung up between trees. Beneath the flag two kids in swimsuits are jumping a sprinkler. As I pass a rainbow traces up and down the spray. School must be out. Why don't you stay home from school, Jackson said. Hang out with me. You're so smart you barely need to show up anyhow. Will I get in trouble? Not if you say you're sick, he said—his hand on my face, under my shirt, showing me where to touch and touching me until the walls were gone, windows doors roof dropping away and everything open space light pouring liquid.

Bits of cotton drift toward the windshield like snowflakes, shadows from the trees making patterns on the road in front of me, like afternoons in the bedroom when the breeze made a movie on the wallpaper, rows of white daisies with yellow centers on a green background, shadow and light shifting like words or music trying to tell me something important, moving across the flowers with their yellow centers while Jackson's fingers stroked my hair. I'm an adult almost, Jackson said, and you are, too. As soon as your mother did what she did, you became an adult. Listen Michael, there's a canyon in Arizona a mile deep with caves and hidden places where no one can find you. And at the top of the Earth in Sweden is a hotel made of ice. I'm going to live in one of those places. I just need to decide what's easier, always needing to warm up or always needing to cool off.

Jackson's body. The feel of him the safest place on Earth, the safest.

The last turn is so sudden I almost miss it. The old man said, If you don't make the turn you'll end up on the road down with the police car waiting in a pull-off. I make the turn and follow the signs for BATTLES, POINT PARK, INCLINE TRAIN. Step number three is the last one he knows about. He thinks step number four is taxi to Greyhound. But I will be taking a taxi the other way. Across the river to the *Delta Queen*, docked beside the park.

Two more curves and there's the Incline Railway gift shop, and behind it the platform sticking out over the edge of the cliff: WORLD'S STEEPEST MILE BUILT 1895. I park in the last visitor's space and leave the keys under the seat like he told me. Jeremy works at the fudge counter, he said. Should have a name tag. He's got arm tattoos and gauge earrings. Say the Watchman sent you. Don't forget to tell him about the van.

There's the train car hanging from cables at the top of the tracks. He said they took Zeke to ride it when he was little, but when his wife saw how the seats tip forward so that when you're at the top you're looking straight down the cliff, she wouldn't get on. So he took Zeke alone, down and up again, just the two of them.

On a clear day you can see all the way to the Great Smoky Mountains. But today the sky is white so I can't see anything past downtown, not even the two towers where the river bends and disappears behind the ridge. *Beehives. Two wars. If you tell the president nothing else, you got to tell him this.*

On the glass door a cartoon dog drinks a slushy. NOTICE: PERSONS, BACKPACKS, AND BAGS OF ANY KIND ARE SUBJECT TO INSPECTION PRIOR TO ENTRY. In my backpack are the hard-boiled eggs and bread and wrapped-up potatoes, two plastic bottles of water, the clothes and toilet paper and Barbie toothbrush. And the pills, which I move to an inside pocket in my jacket before stepping inside, just in case. The sudden air-conditioning gives me chill bumps. Smells of popcorn and chocolate and gasoline. Hardly anyone in here, just a man and woman with a little girl, a toddler.

The fudge counter is in the back. I read the labels beneath bread-shaped slices: dark chocolate marshmallow, milk chocolate caramel, white chocolate pecan. On the top shelf are candies shaped like orange slices: blue and green and hot pink, glittery with sugar. There's also a freezer case with pastel domes of ice cream beneath the glass. Each mound smooth as a pearl. I would rather have ice cream. But you can't put that in a bag.

You want a sample, hon?

A woman holds out a tray with bits of fudge sitting on lace paper, a little spread of oil beneath each one. I choose a piece with nuts and let it dissolve on my tongue while pretending to examine polished rocks in a barrel. Picking up one rock, sliding it into a velvet bag and taking it out again. Like I'm undecided. Like, if you're going to buy a colored rock, you'd better be sure which. No Jeremy. The security camera in the corner is something I didn't consider and probably the old man didn't either, because who would be looking for me here? Maybe I should have left his hat on, or maybe that would look suspicious, wearing a sun hat inside. Sweat stained and crumpled, with the string like a necklace of hard leather knots.

Can I help you find something? the woman asks.

Is Jeremy here?

He's on break. He'll be back in ten minutes.

Okay.

You want me to give him a message?

That's okay. I'll wait.

Tickets are forty dollars and I could just buy one, but would I have to tell my name? And if the panda isn't where I left it I won't have enough. Better to save the forty dollars and wait for Jeremy.

Ten minutes. I turn my back to the camera to look at a wall of painted-glass window hangings: GRANDMA, SISTER, MOTHER. Why would anyone want to hang a sign telling who they are to someone else? Incline Railway key chains, Incline Railway pocketknives, Incline Railway license plates. Aaron, Abby, Adele. Zachary, Zoe. So many Michaels in the middle. T-shirts with a picture of the train hanging from its cables: DON'T LOOK DOWN. Behind the ticket counter a machine swirls stuffing for the foxes and skunks and hedgehogs and beavers hung up by their necks: Build your own forest animal! A man with a shaved head comes out from the back and I see the gauge earrings, and the name tag.

I need a ticket, I say.

One-way or round-trip? Jeremy says.

One-way.

He punches the screen.

The Watchman said to ask you for it.

And now Jeremy is really looking at me.

Holy shit, that guy's still alive?

His van's out front, I say.

Fuuuuck. How'd you wind up with him?

The keys are under the mat, I say—feeling desperate, wishing he wouldn't have told me this plan.

He's a nutjob, that guy. But he's decent. Helped me out when I was trying to get clean. I used to be friends with his son.

Under the mat, I say again, thinking I could have just driven myself. Should have.

Wait here, Jeremy says.

He goes over to the fudge counter, probably to tell the woman, who will call the police. Or maybe he'll call the police himself. I could run out to the van and drive myself. Who cares if he gets his car back. But if they're calling the police it's too late, they'll be waiting on the way down. My heart is beating fast and angry now because no way am I going back to foster care and the babies asleep in car seats being dropped off by social workers, the foster father always in a rage. How do you think we're paying for this house? he yelled. The pittance the state gives. It's time you did your part, Michael. Other girls we've taken in understand their privilege, understand how they must work to earn their keep.

Jeremy over there telling the woman. Any minute now they will be saying, We need you to come with us.

But now he's back and I see what he's holding.

Platform's through those doors, Jeremy says, handing me the white bag. I look inside: a piece of fudge wrapped in paper, and a ticket.

Have a good one, he says, like I'm just any customer.

Out on the platform I stand behind the family with their toddler. In front of them are two old ladies, one with steel-colored hair to her shoulders, the other with white curls like thin cotton balls stuck to her skull. I take a bite of the fudge, plain chocolate melting on my tongue. Above us red numbers on a screen tick down the seconds.

When's *our* turn? The little girl has a tutu pulled over her jeans and sparkly shoes with elastic straps.

Watch the numbers, the mother says. When they get to zero, we can get on.

It's too many numbers! She grips the guardrails, green metal posts close together and bent outward at their tips. The mother lifts her so she can peer through those big binoculars you drop coins into. Directly beneath the platform is a grassy ledge with a birdhouse on a white post. On its shiny black roof SEE ROCK CITY is painted in white letters. The old man said in Rock City they have a thousand-ton rock balanced on the head of a pin. Like an angel flew on down with the rock on his shoulders and just set it there. He said, There are passageways so narrow you gotta turn sideways to get through them, Fat Man's Squeeze, Needle's Eye. A bridge swinging on ropes over a chasm, he said, and a dark cave with peepholes you look through to see fairytale scenes painted in glow-in-the-dark colors. Red Riding Hood's cloak the brightest red you ever seen, he said. How I would love to get me some of that kind of paint.

A chime sounds and we begin to board. The aisle steps are steep and carpeted. Tall windows on all sides and even the roof is made of glass. The family sits in the front row on one side, the old women in the front row on the other side. I choose a seat halfway back.

I'm sliding! the little girl cries.

Here, hold on to this.

I'm gonna fall!

You won't fall.

I'm gonna fall down into the sky!

Some flat white tops of buildings are directly below us, and tall glinting buildings to the left where the river curves toward the bridges. But if I look straight out in front of me, it's just sky and far-off mountains. Lighter in the distance, darker up close, until the darkest-green ridge on the other side of the highway. A hawk hangs in midair, swaying side to side like it's waiting for the train to drop so it can close its wings and fall with us. I look straight down and feel my stomach drop and that place between my legs going soft. I'll only rub on the outside, Jackson said. I promise I would never do anything that would make you feel unsafe. You shouldn't be scared. You're thirteen. A lot of girls your age do this.

The hawk swaying there in the faded sky.

A jolt and the train loosens. The little girl screams and her mother holds her against her shoulder so the girl's panicked eyes are looking back at me. We begin to slide, slowly. If we weren't hooked to the cable above the tracks we'd fly down like this was a ski slope. We slip into the shade between cliffs, a sudden cooling, jagged wet rocks on either side with thin waterfalls trickling from cracks, pillows of moss and strands of ivy dangling down like those party toys that blow out streamers.

A recorded voice crackles in the overhead speaker: *Beautiful Lookout Mountain, the southernmost extension of the Appalachian plateau, is a ninety-mile-long*

ridge spanning the length of three states. Three miles in
Tennessee, thirty-five miles in Georgia, and fifty-two
miles in Alabama. At present, we are twenty-one hundred
feet above sea level, descending at a rate of six hundred
feet per minute.

So I am two states away from the old man now.
And soon will be a mile down. And when he wakes he
will know I thought about him because of the note and
the potatoes.

With a 72.7 percent grade at the top, the Incline
Railway has the distinction of being the steepest pas-
senger railway in the world.

I brought the pajamas you got me for Christmas,
one of the old women says.

Which color did I get you?

They're my travel pajamas.

They're too big for you, aren't they? Size large is
too big.

It doesn't matter. I like them a lot.

Fastest way down the mountain, taking doctors and
nurses to work when the roads ice over. The Incline has
even ensured that mothers in labor make it to the hospital.

We come out of the rocky part and the track starts to
level out, our chairs tipping backward until we're sitting
up like normal. Kudzu all around, hiding who knows
what beneath. A telephone pole coming every few feet.
I count four seconds between them. We pass a shack
with quilts laid out for sale, and a section of run-down

houses. A small white house slides right up against the track and in the window I see a girl with a towel on her head. She's facing us, smiling and waving. Like she's been waiting for us to pass. Imagine living that close to the track, all these strangers looking into your window.

In front of you is Missionary Ridge, where Chattanooga became known as the Gateway to the South.

The station at the bottom has a black-and-white awning, and the American and Tennessee flags flapping on poles. The Tennessee flag reminds me of the flag with the X tacked above the bed where Jackson and me did what we did.

Did you pack tennis shoes?

You told me not to pack tennis shoes.

Everyone packs tennis shoes.

At the bottom of the track is an ice-cream shop with a giant lit-up cone on the roof. Triple scoop: pink, green, and yellow. Cherry on top.

Ice cream coooooone! the little girl yells.

The mother and father are gathering their things.

I'm sorry we were so loud, the mother says. Do you live here?

I go to school here, I say.

We're trying to decide between the aquarium and the children's museum, the mother says. Which do you think would be better for her?

I'm not sure, I say. I get off quickly and follow the arrows painted on the sidewalk. GIFT SHOP THIS WAY.

More cameras, but it's the only way out to the parking
lot where the taxis are waiting. And there's a small bus:
CARTA, Chattanooga's free electric shuttle.

Does this go to Coolidge Park?

The driver is eating a sandwich.

Nope, the driver says. Turnaround's at the aquarium. But you can get off there and walk across the Walnut
Street Bridge.

When does this bus leave?

The driver checks her watch.

Six minutes, she says.

Why didn't the old man tell me about the free
shuttle? Then I remember: he thinks step four is taxi to
Greyhound station. But the shuttle is better. I can keep
the taxi money to add to what's in the panda. Because I
don't know how much it will cost in Washington, DC.

All of us knew about the three kinds of states. None
of us on birth control. Some girls pregnant and King
happy about it, another child in the system. But Jessamine said, You should know where to go, just in case.

The first kind of state is: Your state requires that
one of your parents give permission; a judge can excuse.
The second kind is: Your state requires that one of your
parents be told of your decision forty-eight hours before;
a judge can excuse. Anywhere you could drive or hitch-
hike, you would need a parent's permission or else would
have to go to a judge.

But there's a third kind of state: No parental involvement necessary.

Those states are: Connecticut, Hawaii, Maine, New York, Oregon, Vermont, Washington—and Washington, DC. Which isn't a state and is the easiest in the whole country because anyone can do it, even someone who's not a doctor. So maybe it's not a coincidence the old man is sending me there. Maybe God has different rules for different people, like there are different rules for different states.

Two lines saying yes. But what if it was Jackson's? Sometimes I trick myself into thinking it's his, to find out what I would do. And what I find out is that I would still go to Washington. I would go even if he was the one who put it there.

I board the shuttle and in my head I cross off *taxi to boat*. Imagine writing instead *shuttle + walk across bridge to boat*. Which will take a little more time.

On the bench across from me is a man with a little dog in his lap, the smashed-nose bulging-eyes kind. The man has on red sneakers and red-rimmed glasses, and the dog has on a red bow tie, so they look like a family on their way to take pictures. I'm feeling sick from the fudge and the swaying train car, but I'm still hungry. Unzip the backpack and reach inside to finger-open the foil packet with the soft potatoes, cold and watery now. I have to eat enough to be not-hungry but not too much or I'll be sick like the day the blind man came. That was the day I counted how long since the last time I had it.

If food could stop in my own stomach and not get transferred to the other. Bodies should be able to stay separate. Because it's not Jackson's not mine not even real yet. And in Washington, DC, if you have enough money, you can get drugs to not feel anything. But I have the old man's pills just in case.

I eat four potato slices and sip some water and then the bus is whirring out of the lot past the ice-cream shop, where I see the little girl and her parents sitting at a picnic table beneath a pink-striped umbrella. We go under an overpass with graffiti and cut over to Market Street, which King always took across to the other side of the river where the *Delta Queen* is docked beneath the Market Street Bridge. So I know the way from here.

Pass the section of apartment buildings that look like the ones in College Park in Atlanta, where I used to live with my mother and all night long the airplanes were loud and her boyfriends were coming and going, the two of us changing apartments every few months until the last place we lived, where she left me at Carla's whenever the boyfriends came. Carla's door was on the balcony across from ours. At least she took you to the neighbor's first, Jackson said, when I told him what she did. On one side of our apartment was a boy so small he needed shots to grow, and downstairs was a boy whose mother lived in a wheelchair, her body slumped and getting stiffer by the second. She's going to freeze up slowly, the boy said, all the way down to her lungs and heart and then she'll be dead and buried.

The shuttle makes a stop in front of the restaurant shaped like a triangle on the corner of King Street. You know what's special about this city? King said once. They've got a Martin Luther King Street like everywhere else, but they've also got a plain King Street. One a preacher who let himself get killed, the other a ruler with real power. No preacher ever fixed any of the world's problems. Jesus and Gandhi and Martin Luther King spoke from within the system and got themselves killed. A real king ignores the system. A real king goes behind the system and works to undermine it.

Two teenage girls get on. They're holding phones and coffees and have little purses strapped across their chests. Oh my *God*, look at your *dog*, one of them says to the man. He lifts the dog's paw and makes him do a wave.

Say hello, Paulo, he says.

Paulo, Paulo! the girls cry. We move forward and the dog blinks and licks at the breeze coming through the half-lowered windows. I am on my way to Washington. I will do the steps. And then will come the wide-open space on the other side, Grand Canyon or ice hotel or maybe both. Or maybe come back to see the old man once more. To say thank you.

The girls tap on their phones and hold them up to show one another. To live like that—to have always lived like that, to not have this problem. To stay in the house with Jackson I had to ride to Chattanooga Tuesdays and keep taking the floating pills. Once a day at first for the good feeling, then twice a day, then two pills twice a day or else the vomiting and diarrhea would start, and the chills and sweating and not being able to sleep. Just ride to the *Delta Queen* one day a week, take extra pills at the gas station on the Georgia-Tennessee border. Sandpaper-man, Panda-man, Oldy-man. Sometimes, on other days, there were johns in Macon. Fast and easy and didn't pay as much. But make the drive to the rich johns, King said, and I could live there with my own room and new clothes. The foster father taking half the money and Jackson doing with new girls what he did with me.

We don't have to if you don't want to, Jackson said, if you don't want me to—

I do want you to.

Are you sure?

Yes.

Right here, is that where—

Yes.

I don't want to hurt you.

It's not.

I can tell it hurts.

It doesn't, please Jackson—

I'll just rub on the outside, tell me if it hurts.

Doing it like that and his body the safest. Until one day not looking at me. Sitting on the edge of his bed, voices in the hallway and then Jessamine coming in, and a short man with a beard the color of an old penny.

Hello there, gorgeous, the man said. She's a beauty just like you said.

I've been hearing about you, he said to me, how beautiful and how smart. I've been hoping to meet you. And here you are right in front of me.

I cover myself with blankets. Jackson looking at the walls, at his feet, not looking at me.

He wants to take you on a date, Michael, Jessamine said. A nice date.

That's an interesting name, the man said. Michael. You named after your daddy?

She's named after an angel, Jessamine said. The most powerful angel in the Bible.

Oh, that is perfect, the man said. Yes, we'll call you Angel.

My name is Michael, I said. All of me shaking now, and Jackson leaving, closing the door behind him.

You should be happy he wants to give you a nick-name, Jessamine said.

She doesn't want me to call her that, it's her busi-ness, the man said.

He pressed his hands together like he was praying; dark tattoos on the outsides of his palms met to make the shape of a crown.

See if you can guess my name, he said.

I don't care what your name is.

Oh, she's got fight. That's good. Listen, Michael, how about the four of us go out? Me and Jessamine and you and Jackson. I know a restaurant where they have white tablecloths and gold forks and knives. You can order anything you like. Here, look what I bought for you. This will look beautiful on you with those long legs. Where'd you get such legs? It is obvious you are special. Different than any other girl I've met.

Jackson coming in to get his backpack, not looking at me. Jackson, I said, but he left again and I heard the screen flap shut behind him *snap-snap*.

The electric shuttle turns onto Broad Street into the shade of the tall buildings. Down here there's a stop at every cross street. The bank clock on the corner says 12:57, the bus to Washington is 3:20, and that leaves enough time for *walk across bridge to boat*. I've seen the Walnut Street Bridge at night from the riverboat deck. In winter they put up electric snowflakes that blink on and off all night, and in the summer American flags with red stripes that light up one by one, like an invisible hand underlining sentences. I've never walked across, only looked at it from the *Delta Queen*.

The bus stops in front of a theater with light bulbs chasing the *Seussical*. A lineup of children climb on. Wide eyes in heads that seem too big for their bodies. The teachers get them settled and we are moving again. Now come the glass triangles on the aquarium roof, pyramids leaning into one another, like they're propping each other up. A whole jungle inside that glass, Jessamine told me, with butterflies that will land on your finger. Why are there butterflies in an aquarium? I asked. It's like the sky above the ocean, she said.

The man and Paulo get off beside the wall with colored nubs and people on ropes climbing to the top to ring a red bell. We pull into the plaza in front of the aquarium. The last stop. I sip some water and eat an egg while the children get off in their buddy pairs. I get off last and follow some pretend train tracks that lead to the pedestrian bridge. On the concrete between the tracks are the words:

> *Got-ta keep it rollin'*
> *Shov-el all the coal in*
> *you know that Ten-nes-see is not very-y far*
> *When you hear the whis-tle blow-in' eight to*
>   *the bar*

But the lyrics are coming backward. So the tracks must lead to the aquarium, not away from it.

At Market Street the light is red. I wait, listening to children on the water steps leading down to the river. TRAIL OF TEARS BEGINS HERE. I remember this from school, how the people forced to leave were told there would be a boat waiting. But it was a lie, there was no boat and they had to walk out across the prairie and everyone died in the heat.

Beside me is a statue of a mermaid. Her shirt is parted like curtains and shows a triangle of belly, her hair frozen and wild around her sad face, sad like my mother's face when she took me to Carla's apartment on the balcony across. *Carla has a jelly bean jar, you can have as many as you like. I don't want jelly beans, where are you going? Nowhere, I just need some rest. Is it a boyfriend? Yes, it's a boyfriend.* I stood at the window looking across to our door where my mother was inside, no longer protected by me. Carla's hand on my back circling over and over, like the hand was saying, It's okay, it's okay. At bedtime she made up the couch and I closed my eyes but only to where the lashes shivered so I could see between them like looking through a screen door. Carla watching the TV where people kept laughing, her hands pinching her arms and legs and face, then going up to her head, braiding and unbraiding her hair and starting over with her arms and legs. Doing everything in circles.

Waking to flashing blue-red, blue-red and the police at the door.

Are you the babysitter? We are looking for her son.

What is it, what happened?

Left a note on the counter. Addressed to Michael. Probably best for him not to read.

Michael's her daughter, what happened, what happened?

At the Market Street intersection the green WALK sign lights up. I go fast up the hill toward the white pillars of the museum and the sculpture of a horse made of sticks. The old man said he would never sell to galleries or museums, no matter how much they offered for his paintings. The Lord shown me that people are coming from New York City, he said, who want to buy all this here art and put it in a gallery. But my cabin is the gallery, see? Holy Spirit can't do his work in city museums and galleries.

In front of me a woman struggles to push a wide stroller up the hill and when I pass her I can see the big numbers on her watch: 1:22. As long as I am on the way to the Greyhound by 2:30, 2:45 latest. Hot and dizzy and thirsty, too. Signs pointing every direction:

RIVERFRONT. WALNUT STREET BRIDGE. BLUFF VIEW ART DISTRICT. HUNTER MUSEUM.

My breath comes hard at the top of the hill, but here is the pedestrian bridge now with a statue of a dog as tall as a human, lifting its paw, welcoming people to cross. I need to pee and there's another ice-cream place here, the mix-in kind. Enough time.

Inside it's cool with an overhead fan blowing currents of air. The restrooms are down a hallway past a counter stacked with waffle cones. Locked. CUSTOMER USE ONLY.

I get in line behind a woman wearing a dress to her ankles.

I got you each your own! a girl says. She looks my age. She hands out cups with swirls of white and

sprinkles to three little boys wearing identical rocket
ship T-shirts.

I *love* your dress, the girl behind the counter says
to the woman in front of me.

Thank you very much, the woman says.

You're supposed to choose vanilla or chocolate and
then a machine mixes in whatever you decide. Seventeen-
thousand possible flavors. I saved $12 taking the free
shuttle and the small size with one topping mixed in is
$4.99 so even after ice cream I'll still be ahead. Behind
the counter are tall clear tubes with cereals and nuts
and sprinkles and gummies and crushed-up cookies and
cakes. Seventeen-thousand is how it should be. Nothing
to think about but which colors to buy. *It's color that will
save you, Michael*, my mother said. *Not religion. Red
orange and yellow will wake up your need, green blue
and purple will satisfy it. Religions are myths invented
by men to keep power away from women, but even when
you recognize this you will not be able to save yourself.
You will lose everything but you will never lose blue.*
Once she took me to the part of Atlanta where the houses
were painted in blues and yellows and greens and even
pinks, so we could look again at the one we chose as our
favorite, the one we named the English Tea House with
hydrangeas along a picket fence and a stone pathway
to the front door. *I want you to see what normal looks
like, Michael. Sleeping in a car and moving apartments
every few months is not normal. All of these people*

went to college. Whatever you do in this life you must promise me you will never quit school. Say it. I need you to promise. But I couldn't say it because her hands were squeezing my shoulders so hard and shaking me so my teeth knocked together. *I will tell you what it means to be a woman. At night you lie awake and plan the things you will do the next day. Make a good breakfast with some eggs, wash and sweep up, go out and find a job. Then morning comes and you cannot do any of those things. A woman who makes plans will always fail.*

What you are doing, Michael, King said, will get you everything other people struggle for years to achieve. Just take your pills and do your job at the *Delta Queen* once a week and you can have everything. King said that if I wanted to, I could go to school. But school and teachers and other students began to move backward, I could see them all there in front of me but if I ran for twenty miles I couldn't touch them, I was on one side of a screen and everyone who wasn't Jackson King or Jessamine was on the other side. Until one day nothing on the other side seemed normal anymore.

But now I am making plans. Her fault I have to. Dying on purpose. Stopping her own heart. And him with his barely beating heart and his lung coughing up blood, back there dying but trying so hard not to. Maybe awake now and thinking I am taking his visions to Washington, DC, where anyone even someone not a doctor can do it, not a coincidence—

Someone behind me taps my shoulder.

Sorry, I say.

Vanilla with sprinkles, I say to the salesgirl. Which is not what I want.

The girl pulls first one lever then another and the mixture swirls into a cup. I ask for the bathroom key. Dangling from the cherry on a plastic ice-cream cone. When I finish in the restroom my ice cream is sitting on the counter, a swirled peak in liquid. Above the register, a clock reads 1:45. Hurry now.

Back outside and here is the walking bridge. And once I'm across, I will be to step five: Get panda.

Three bridges cross the river. Two for cars and the middle one just for people. The middle bridge is made of old wooden planks with metal arches above. At the entrance, the black dog's lifted paw. I rub the smooth spot on its knuckle where the gold shows through, then walk fast eating the soupy ice cream and spitting out the sprinkles, leaving a trail and telling myself, Don't look left. But still I can hear the cars crossing Market Street Bridge, making their three notes, *ahhhh-ohhhh-ahhhh*, and even without looking I can picture the *Delta Queen* docked there beneath. An old-fashioned riverboat that once carried famous people up and down America's rivers—three presidents and a man who walked on the moon—with carved wooden staircases and marble-floored bathrooms, restaurants, and bars with thick velvet drapes and gas lanterns flickering on tables. All that money to build a boat now left to rot down there beside the park. Empty cabins with mattresses on rusted bed frames, worn-down couches and cobwebs and mouse droppings. I used the room with a plaque on the door: HER ROYAL HIGHNESS PRINCESS MARGARET. A queen's sister who came all the way from England to ride the boat, her trip down the Mighty Mississippi mostly forgotten after her death. Framed above the bed is a letter I have read over and over. Signed by Lord someone, Kensington Palace. *Want you to know what a very great pleasure it gave Her Royal Highness Princess Margaret to spend three hours aboard the* Delta Queen.

The arches above me tick past one by one, wooden planks below worn away in places. Every so often, a peephole big enough to catch a flash of the water below. Don't look left. *Ahhhh-ohhhh-ahhhh.* The *ohhhh* is the middle part where the bridge opens to let tall ships pass, but I've never seen it open, never seen a single big ship on this river, only speedboats and kayaks and people standing on surfboards paddling downstream. My stomach tugs inward, too much sugar and not enough to drink. Heat wrinkling the air, warping the arches.

I throw what's left of the ice cream into a trash can. Sit on a bench and drain one of the water bottles. Everything inside me feeling like it's trying to come up. Not yet not yet, I tell it.

Stand and walk until the bridge starts to go downhill a little. So I have passed halfway. There's the golden

horse on top of the carousel, the spinning weather vane
kind, all its legs pulled up running—the wind making it gallop north, away from downtown, away from
Georgia and Alabama and the mountain. I turn around
to see how far I've come. The front of the mountain
comes to a point like a ship sailing into Tennessee. Horse
and mountain both charging north and stuck in place.

I have beat you, horse.

I have beat you, mountain.

The bridge ends at Frazier Avenue, with all the shops
and restaurants. Hurry. But maybe I should eat a slice of
bread to soak up the ice cream? Or maybe that would
be worse. Only two more steps and I will be on the bus.
Get on the right bus. Stay on. In the shop windows are
slouchy bags with leather fringe, necklaces with charms
in the shapes of states, Christmas tree ornaments made
of stained glass. Between shops is an alleyway with steps
leading down to a parking lot and the long stretch of
Coolidge Park. Beyond that, planks to board the *Delta
Queen*.

Graffiti covers the brick alley. *Dios Te Ama. Queer
Liberation. Watch out for the glow-in-the-dark CIA.* I
am running now—down the steps, across the parking lot.
But no. Don't run, don't attract attention. Walk don't run
past the fountain where brass turtles and elephants and
pigs spit streams of water onto wet children. Walk don't
run across the grass between me and edge of the water.
And then I can't not look anymore: there's the riverboat

in the sunlight, a rotting layer cake with its lacy frosting
of balconies and a black candle stuck on top. The big red
paddle in back, and the row of gold whistles that gasp out
circus songs. When it was dark out you could imagine how
a queen's sister must have seen it. *Would like to express
her deepest thanks. Marvelous example of a riverboat,
capturing the magnificence of a bygone age upon the Mississippi River.* But in the daylight you see the truth: the
peeling paint and sagging decks, and on the second level,
the roped-off rooms marked UNDER RENOVATION.

And I know that nothing on that level is being
renovated.

Alongside the boat is a blue-railed boardwalk. Tall
wavy grasses and rocks all the way down to the water,
which is calm-seeming on the top, with currents below
that King said would pull you under and keep you there.

Down near the put-in for kayaks, babies appear
and disappear, little heads bobbing in and out of sight.
Abs in tight! a woman's voice yells. Add the lower body!

Now I see the mothers squatting down and lifting
the babies like weights.

Feel that burn!

Two planks go from the boardwalk to the boat.
One is for guests, the other for employees. I always used
the employees' plank at night. But today I am a guest. I
could be just any tourist. It's been almost a month and
probably no one will recognize me with my hair short
and no blond wig. There are white and pink balloons tied

to the rails of the rear deck. Some kind of party going on. I could be coming here for the party.

So many reasons a person might come here.

Jessamine told me, When you step onto the boat the performance begins. Remember, you are the star but sometimes you won't feel like it, and you will have to come outside of yourself, you will have to become the audience watching yourself up on a stage. We all learned to do it and you will too—getting out of the car, practicing floating up to look down at the girl in a blond wig walking across the plank and opening the double doors, climbing two flights of stairs and lifting her chin as she steps into the Texas Lounge. Low leather couches and gas flames flickering in lanterns, stained glass almonds in windows circling the room like pairs of yellow cat eyes. Watch the girl walk up to the bar, the edge cushioned with leather. Watch her sit facing the framed photograph of an old president taking a tour up and down the Mississippi, and beside it a picture of the first female captain who lived and died on the *Delta Queen* and now haunts Room 109. In the picture the woman is frowning, gripping the wheel with both hands, like someone maybe said, You cannot be a boat captain, and she said, *Watch*. She owned the boat, Panda-man told me once. She was never a real captain. Watch this girl pretending not to notice Panda-man, whose contract says she must act, every week, as if it's the first time they've met. Hello there, beautiful, may I buy you a drink? Watch the bartender play along because the tips from these men pay his rent and tuition. Watch the bartender watching the man take the girl's arm and lead her to the back stairs, the girl overly confident in her high heels. The girl knows that the bartender knows. That he sometimes considers making a call. She knows his reasoning, too: most of the women who work here do so by choice. Not a crime, if it's by choice. This girl who comes Tuesdays looks healthy. Happy, even. No discernible bruises. He's never asked her age. She could be legal.

Now, in the daytime, the watching eyes in the Texas Lounge are lit golden by sunlight. Tables with chairs pushed in and the bar at the back with velvet drapes closed over the liquor shelves. Stifling heat and the squeezing in my belly, my throat tight, too, and if it comes up now it will make a loud noise and attract attention. I go to the restroom, lock the door and sit on the lid. Take out two of the pain pills. Just holding them in my hand makes the peaceful feeling wash over. Two will make me sleepy but one will make me calm. I swallow one and put the other back. Take out the piece of paper with the steps, tear off the ones I've already done and flush them down. So now my list says only what's left: Get panda. Take taxi to Greyhound station. Get on the bus and stay on. Step eight.

I didn't write down step eight in case the old man or anyone else saw. But I know what goes in the blank space after the number. Panda Taxi Greyhound Eight.

Panda Taxi Greyhound Eight. Say it till my breathing gets slow. Through the open bathroom window I can hear the water slosh against the side of the boat. The Chattanooga Ducks tour guide is talking on a speaker, telling the history. MoonPie, Coca-Cola. Sold the original bottling rights for one dollar.

Hurry. To get to the lifejackets I will have to go to the outside staircase and down a flight to where the rooms are, the ones supposedly being renovated. Where the room with the plaque is. My breathing slower my throat opening up. But exhausted, suddenly. Tired of my heart beating and the smaller one beating too. But not attached to me. Put there by what I didn't choose. By what King chose, or maybe Jesus. Maybe Jesus chose.

Below me on the big rear deck are tables laid out with plates and silverware and trays of food, bottles in silver buckets, balloons tied to the railing where women in pink sequined cowboy hats are posing for a photo. The one in the middle has a phone on a stick. Behind them the fat concrete legs of the bridge rising to the *ohhhh* in the middle, the river bending and disappearing, heading to where it joins the Mississippi all the way to the Delta, which is haunted by Confederate soldiers trying to find their way home. That's a legend, Panda-man said, there's no such thing as ghosts. Angel, come here Angel, that's good. Listen, the Mississippi is a mighty river not in itself but because it is all the creeks and streams and rivers running down from Canada combined, becoming bigger than its container, splitting the land wide-open and spilling out calm as bathwater into the Gulf in Florida where our vacation home—no, leave that on, don't ever show me your real—in Naples where my in-laws are, so that's where we, I mean it made sense to buy—yes, right there, ahhhh. I am a damaged man, Angel, a deeply troubled man, what I am doing is tantamount to murder but you have become essential to me, to my well-being and if I can find a way to provide you with means, get you a nice place, maybe even Naples—ahhh ohhh—God, fuck, Angel—my angel—

How about Sweden? I say. How about the Grand Canyon? But now his hand shoves harder, hairs gray and black on his flat stomach, till the sound in my throat pushes him out. Turn over now, he says, and I do and feel it hot all over my back. The only john who never did it inside. Who put extra in the panda purse hidden along the walkway past the wooden door with the plaque and the letter from Kensington Palace above the bed. *She was most beautifully looked after.* But now I pass the door and feel nothing because of the nice floating feeling, the best feeling in the world, like everything is okay, everything is right, I will do anything anyone tells me to.

How I have missed this feeling.

Last bench on the right. I kneel and lift the lid to feel all the life vests stacked flat, probably never

used. Reach all the way back to feel for the plush—still
there!—my hand closes around it, feeling the tight line
of the zipper.

Thinner than it should be.

Can I help you?

A woman in a vest with a badge: DELTA QUEEN STAFF.

I'm fine, I say, clutching the panda purse.

Too thin.

Her eyes go up and down.

Are you here with the party?

Yeah, I say. I should get back.

What'd you have there?

Just my sister's toy.

I stuff the panda in my pocket. Do not look behind.
Thinner than it should be. My stomach can't hold it
anymore and I could make it to the bathroom but I
need to get off the boat in case the lady with the visor
is following. Down the stairs to the main deck, out the
wood doors while the steam whistles start up, jog-walk
across the park with the song echoing against the cliffs
across the river, *Goin' to the Chapel* in two different keys.
I glance back and see the women lifting their drinks,
the woman in the red vest or someone dressed like her
holding a tall cake, *gon-na get ma-a-a-ried*, the whistles
hoarse like the boat is sick sick like my stomach like him
in the night coughing wheezing but still taking care of
me making sure I had food and no one found me. Safe

in a mighty fortress. Lost and now found. Hold it in just a little longer, up the stairs into the alleyway with the graffiti where there is no one.

Potatoes and egg and ice cream and water splatter the chalk on the sidewalk.

Shady here. I let myself sink with my back to the wall. Put my hand in the pocket and feel the panda's stomach where the zipper is buried. Where every week I crumpled a hundred-dollar bill and put it inside until the panda was fat with stuffing.

Inside is a pamphlet, folded. On the cover is a drawing of a cross casting a shadow onto a kneeling woman.

Oakview Rescue Mission. For immediate assistance text *Are You Awake* to the number below.

Trauma-informed, biblically sound, two-year rent-free commitment healing safety restoration.

On the back a handwritten note:

Angel, I hope you are reading this. Tonight they brought a different girl and I can abide myself no longer. I am turning myself in. Call this number. You won't have to worry about anything, not money, not social services. Will make sure your pimp is prosecuted to the fullest extent of the law.

Maybe one thousand dollars before. Two twenties now, folded crisp. To force me to call. I tear up the pamphlet. I still have enough for the bus ticket. In Washington I will figure out where to get more.

Just get to Washington.

I run to Frazier Avenue and stand there with my thumb out. Almost immediately, a car pulls up.

Hey, baby, where you going?

A woman in glasses and blue nurse clothes. Empty car seat in back.

The Greyhound station, I say. By the airport?

Ten bucks I take you there, twenty I won't remember I did it, the woman says.

I hand her a twenty and she does a zipper on her lips.

I'm Millicent, she says when I get in.

Sarah, I say.

Good to meet you, Sarah, she says.

The dashboard clock says 2:54. I will make it if there's no traffic. We take the bridge across Market Street and when we reach the middle I can feel the *ahhhh-ohhhh-ahhhh* vibrate in my chest. The floating pill feeling so good now. I will save the other pill for the bus. The woman is not talking, not asking anything, and I am so grateful I push my face against the window to press back the crying.

Crying because I have done all the steps. Almost all.

You hungry baby? the woman says. You want to stop and get something to eat?

I'm trying to catch a bus, I say.

I got you, she says. The car speeds up and she opens the compartment between us.

At least have one of these, she says, handing me a granola bar.

The salty-sweet gets rid of the throw up taste. I wrap up the other half and put it in my backpack. Lean my head against the window and let my eyes close for the first time since his coughing spitting smell of paint and woodsmoke sun turning the rose petals pink and him saying Good morning, Michael . . .

Hand on my arm.

Hey, baby. We're here.

3:26.

Too late—

I don't want to make trouble for you, the woman says, but I gotta ask if you want to call someone?

She's holding out a cell phone. *Are You Awake*. Won't have to worry about anything. Not money, not law.

Inches away.

No thanks, I say.

Tell you what, then, she says. You keep this.

She gives me back the twenty. I stuff it into my pocket and get out. Before I close the door she leans over.

When you get where you're going, she says, you remember Miss Millicent did you a kindness, and you—

But I am leaving her behind, running to the entrance because maybe the bus hasn't left yet and *all you got to do is get on and stay on* all the way to Washington, DC, to step eight, which now that I have made it to Greyhound I can let myself think.

A woman who makes plans.

Planned planned planned.

The place I need to go before I can go anywhere else.

Gospel

> In sleep
> The dreamer wakes. He sees
> Above the stars the deep
> Of Heaven opened. Is
>
> He living, then, his part
> Of Heaven's earthly life?
> And what shall be the art
> By which this sight can live?
>
> —Wendell Berry, "Sabbath Poem"
> (after the painting *Jacob's Dream*
> by William Blake and
> Genesis 28:11–17)

> Sed heu, pauci sunt qui in morte proximis
> suis fideliter assistunt, interrogando,
> monendo, et pro ipsis orando.
>
> —*The Ars Moriendi*

May 19, 2014. Alabama backwoods. Cabin interior.

3:26 p.m. (too late!)

The PROPHET is asleep on an inflatable raft, a plate of cooked potatoes and an oil lamp beside him. Facing the mattress is a worn velour recliner and side table. A guitar rests against the table leg. Eleven circular saw blades painted like eyeballs lean against one wall. Upstage is a tree trunk painted with vines, with a wood-burning stove beside it. Crouched beside the stove is TWO-STEP DEVIL. He wears a cowboy hat, denim shirt with snap closures, and skinny jeans tucked into silver-toed cowboy boots. Downstage are a lawn chair, scattered gardening tools, and two high-backed rockers, one with the name MICHAEL painted on.

Lights up.

One

TWO-STEP (*comes downstage, removes his hat, bows deeply*):   Greetings, fleshsacks! (*Replaces hat.*) So about the name. Two-Step. What a shame the old man came up with it, soon he'll be dead and the name will die with him. (*Walks over to crouch beside the Prophet; mimes stroking his hair.*) The Watchman, how he charms me! I want to sleep in his guts and twine myself round his limbs, woo him with soft caresses. The Last Magnificent with his paints and his vegetables and enough belief in eternity to take the rest of you with him. How little he understands his power down here in this no-name spot near the bottom of the North American continent, these hot noisy woods, this smoke-smelling cabin. Blood and shit and sweat, how sweet the incense in my nostrils.

The PROPHET coughs, rolls over. TWO-STEP toes his shoulder with the tip of his boot.

TWO-STEP: Ahem. Ahem.

PROPHET (*jolting up*):   Is it you?

TWO-STEP: C'est moi, Monsieur Magnifique!

PROPHET: Hoo-whee. You're pretty realistic for a dream. Forgot what it feels like to breathe thisaway.

TWO-STEP: Excuse me, but you said, Is it you? I assumed you meant myself. We have been in one another's orbit for quite some time but have never been properly introduced.

PROPHET: I said what?

TWO-STEP: Is it you.

PROPHET: Is it who?

TWO-STEP: Precisely.

PROPHET: Guess I don't know what I said. (*Cautiously.*) Could've been thinking of a girl.

TWO-STEP: Ah. (*Bitterly.*) The waif. The runaway.

PROPHET: You know her? Michael?

TWO-STEP: I see her.

PROPHET: Seen her where?

TWO-STEP: See. Present tense. Here. Now.

PROPHET: What day is it?

TWO-STEP (*petulant*):   You haven't even asked who I am.

PROPHET: I was thinking you look like this devil shows up in here time to time. But you don't sound nothing—

TWO-STEP (*monotone*):   Abaddon Apollyon Baal Beelzebub Belial Dagon Mammon Marduk Mastema Memnoch Mephistopheles Moloch Ancient Enemy Hades Evil One Prince of Darkness Father of Lies Tempter Black Mirror God's Hangman Generous Gambler Necessary Minus Mysterious Stranger Number Forty-Four Arnold Friend Lucifer.

PROPHET: Nothing like any Satan I ever heard.

TWO-STEP (*slams table; spotlight*):   I object! *Satan.* The original Hebrew takes an article: *ha*-satan. *The* adversary. A title, not a proper name. Consider the prosecution

and opposition in a legal case. No one accuses the lawyers of the crimes. They are merely carrying out their
roles on behalf of their clients. I, too, am a hireling. At
the mercy of Creator's directives. Same with my sad-sack
younger brother—but we'll get to him later. Or consider the book of Job. Creator was incapable of tempting
humans to sin, so he needed a scapegoat. Please, sir, may
I have permission to tempt the upright man? Permission
granted, mon fils. What a wretched story. Had Job been
a real person, I would have felt sorry for him. Who
hardened Pharaoh's heart? Sent the opposer to enter
King Saul and Judas Iscariot? Creator calls the shots. I
am consigned to obedience. Don't shoot the messenger.
(*Lights fade to black.*)

Two

*The PROPHET and TWO-STEP sit in the center of
the cabin cross-legged, facing one another. The saw
blades painted like eyeballs are now on the floor
between them. During the following, they take turns
stacking the blades, largest to smallest.*

PROPHET: Hoped I'd get to fight him someday. That
other Satan.

TWO-STEP (*monotone*):   The notion of a unified evil
entity called by the name of Satan was a re-visioning of
mytho-historical records by the church fathers in order

to maintain sociopolitical power. Hostile as I may appear to you, I remain a servant of the divine—

PROPHET: See that's what I mean. Using them words. You can't be him.

TWO-STEP: In former days I spoke in a way you could understand. In these last days I speak as I am. How maligned I have been. How deeply, irrevocably maligned.

PROPHET: Sure can breathe better when you and me is talking, though. Not like when the other Satan came around. Figured I'd slash an X in front of him (*Stands to demonstrate.*) like that preacher done. Wish I'd've found the smallest blade. That reminds me. (*Gets Michael's note from beneath his raft.*) She left this. Left me them cooked potatoes, too. Look how nice she draws letters. Loops and swirls.

TWO-STEP reads, frowns. Folds the note in half and stuffs it into his back pocket.

TWO-STEP (*spotlight*):   Calumniated. Most terribly. Though I'm a fan of the representations. The poems and paintings. And plays. A monster in the bowels of the Earth, his lower body frozen in ice, devouring souls as they fall? Splendid. A black poodle leaving little footprints of fire behind? Fabulous. Lucifer flung down from heaven, the other fallen angels surrounding him like dead leaves on the surface of a lake? Triumphant. Though had I been a mere angel—keep in mind, angels are beings without moral sense, they are barely sentient automa-tons, subordinate even to humans—had I been one of them, I would never have come up with the idea to rebel. Or the will. And the snake in Eden, twisted around the tree of the knowledge of good and evil, telling the woman she won't die if she takes a bite? Those artists paid no attention to the text, in which the serpent is not yet belly-bound.

TWO-STEP gets a hammer and begins driving nails into the wall to hang the Ezekiel blades.

PROPHET: Hey. Gimme that note. (*Two-Step takes the note from his pocket and, without turning, drops it. The Prophet picks it up, unfolds and smooths it.*) Says she's coming back. (*Two-Step continues to hammer.*) Says, I promise. (*Continues to hammer.*) You say you seen her somewhere? (*Continues to hammer.*) You seen if she made it to the White House?

TWO-STEP (*spinning around*):   It's *see*, you fool! (*Resumes hammering as lights fade to black.*) See. See. See.

Three

TWO-STEP and the PROPHET sit cross-legged with the circular saw blades between them as before. Three Ezekiel blades now hang on the wall.

TWO-STEP: . . . and as justification for making the adversary an ancient villain, the church fathers cited 1 John 3:8: *The devil has been sinning from the beginning.* The beginning of what? Planet Earth? The appearance of *Homo sapiens*?

PROPHET (*aside*): Liked him better the way he was before. If it even was him.

> *At center stage rear, a movie screen unscrolls and hits the floor with a bang. It is clean-sheet white, five feet square. The screen shows a film of hands shaping clay on a potter's wheel. The shot slowly pans out to reveal that the potter's wheel is a circular saw blade.*

TWO-STEP (*spotlight*): Behold Creator at his wheel. Sculpting mud and clay into (*mocking air quotes*) *Adam*, the *Imago Dei*. Stand, hairless fragile moist one, be slim-jawed and round-skulled, I have given you a brain to rule the planet! But the Hebrew word translated *Adam* also takes an article. *The* adamah. Not a name, a type. The first *Homo sapiens* to erupt from *Homo erectus*, the smallest next step in a billions-of-years-long process, single cell to aquatic creature to land-crawler to biped to ape to hominid to human. They were always already subject to decay. Entropy hardwired into the system. It was only the *anticipation* of death they lacked. I came and whispered the truth in the adamah's ear: Someday you *shall* die. A fraction of a second later, the adamah formed a concept:

I'm inside this body. Everything else is outside. What's outside dies. Thus I, inside this body, shall likewise die.

The first humans did not fall; they rose. *I* lifted them into personhood. Gave them consciousness and turned them into Imagoes Dei.

Scenes from Herzog's Cave of Forgotten Dreams— images of early cave drawings—flash on the screen as TWO-STEP begins to dance in a primal, ritualistic style.

TWO-STEP: Witness the mad rush into caves, the frenetic drawings-in-charcoal to warn offspring, the move from inarticulate sounds to tongue formations to codified systems of language. The beating-out-of-rhythms foot-stomping hand-clapping wild contortions of dance and the upward tilting of faces to ask sun moon and stars, century after century, in millions of ways across millions of lives, the only authentic question you fleshsacks have ever asked. (*Two-Step's voice magnified to the sound of many voices.*) How do we escape it?

Four

On one side of the stage, the PROPHET squats over a metal bucket, pants around his ankles. On the other side, TWO-STEP hurriedly nails, hangs, and arranges Ezekiel blades so they interlock. Five now hang on the wall.

TWO-STEP: What a faulty machine, the fleshsack. Skin holding muscle holding sinew holding bone holding organ, the whole accidentally united lump of matter beset with *need*. Laws, creeds, sermons, prayers, meditation: attempts to curate the instincts. In the hope of pushing back death. Yet always, the inevitable glorious giving-in. (*Movie screen drops with a bang. Faces of historic figures flash in rapid succession, Buddha, Gandhi, Moses, Joan of Arc, Mother Teresa, Martin Luther King.*) A few have managed to control themselves. But what even these—gurus shall we call them?—cannot rid themselves of is the longing for immortality. That's the fuel upon which the human machine runs. Like C. S. Lewis said: Surely we yearn for immortality because once upon a time we were immortals. Just as our hunger proves there exists such a thing as food, though we may not find it, our thirst for the eternal proves there exists such a thing as eternity—and that something or someone has ruined it.

Over the centuries I've stalked monks in cells, sitting in silence, seeing no one. I've whispered wicked blasphemies and rough temptations into their ears. Doused them in terrors and doubts: what Luther called his *anfechtungen* and the monks called the bath of Satan. These unknown sporadic souls destabilize the entropy of the universe. Their simple prayers spread like a flung net to capture children and widows and refugees, addicts and criminals. If enough minds maintained enough belief on

behalf of enough people, the universe, your universe,
would lift itself out of its bondage to decay. Consciousness, after all, is not separate from matter. Consciousness
is matter. Your physical bodies would die into the heaven
you'd made of your minds. You would take the next
step. Evolve from *Homo sapiens* to something beyond.

*The PROPHET steps out of his pants and leaves them
there. Staggers outside with the bowl, dumps it stage
front. Starts to lower himself into his rocker, changes
his mind, and sits in MICHAEL's.*

TWO-STEP (*light slowly illuminating the PROPHET*):   Oh,
my beloved, out here on the margins, doing for the world
what no congress or president or army could ever do.
Believing the old, old story. Could you see yourself as
I do, you would witness a whirling disc flinging itself
outward. A star going supernova, the formation of a
galaxy. The brilliance!

PROPHET (*shielding his eyes*):   Jesus, sweet Jesus! (*Stands,
staggers.*) Michael! Zeke!

Five

*TWO-STEP is on the PROPHET's raft. Wears only
a pair of bikini underwear. Writhes demonstratively,
touching himself.*

TWO-STEP (*frustrated*):   It never works. Pretending to have genitalia. Meanwhile my sad-sack brother is out there with all the means and none of the will. The flaccid egoist. Believe in *me* and you shall be saved, he kept saying. Have faith in *me*. Dragging those out-of-work fishermen around with him. Mythmakers claim he did it to save the sin-stained race. Creator so perfect he could not allow anything or anyone not perfect to be near him. But if one of them could be *absolutely* perfect? Live a faultless life, die, and go to hell and be perfect even there? Who would sign up for such a thing? My brother volunteered. As everyone knows. A willing sacrifice, humbling himself to take on flesh? Listen, I was there when he signed up. I can tell you: his decision was not a noble one.

The PROPHET appears, dressed in a tunic and sandals. For the rest of the scene he plays the role of JESUS.

JESUS: Lemme be one of them fleshsacks.

CREATOR (*voiced by TWO-STEP*):   It will not go well for you.

JESUS: A kind of experiment. What's it like to *feel*?

CREATOR: You will be lonely. You will experience unspeakable pain.

JESUS: Got it, pain and loneliness. But also lust and pride!

CREATOR: You will die.

JESUS: And the experiment will done be over with. I'll
come on back here and carry on like before.

TWO-STEP (*as himself*):   It did not go well for him. The
dying part was fine. He expected it. Was begging for it,
really. He'd had enough of the planet by then. It was what
came after. Waking up and finding himself still in a body
and unable to die a second time. Facing the long centuries
ahead, the same old world with its piddling desires and
petty nostalgias. Would it surprise you to learn that I,
too, asked to become a fleshsack? But Creator refused.
Creator must be the hero. No heroes without adversaries.
I turned out to be the sacrificial lamb. My brother was
expendable. A minor character in the story of the universe,
subordinate to the master narrative of good and evil. So
why not let him have his little adventure?

> *Movie screen hits floor. A planet Earth appears. Inside
> the Earth, something squirms around. The planet
> bulges and swells. A crack appears at the equator,
> snakes down through the continent of Africa. Knuckles
> emerge. Wrist, forearm, elbow. A fist and arm punch-
> ing through the bottom of the planet. The fist comes
> to rest on the belly of a YOUNG GIRL.*

TWO-STEP: And so began the Grand Compression.
Squeezing my brother to the size of a zygote. Why
their plan had to involve fetal development I still don't

understand. That Hebrew girl was warned beforehand by one of the lower-down messengers. As if obtaining the consent of a fourteen-year-old exonerated Creator of the crime! You should have seen the way she kicked and begged when the time came. No one tells that part of the story. Yes, she was a virgin. But her reproductive mechanisms had not yet kicked in. No eggs yet released. This was crucial to the escape plan. Any preexisting flesh material was dangerous. My brother needed to remain immortal. A human incubator was as much as they were willing to risk.

The incessant heartbeat and the horrific pulsing belly cord—I had to look away. And when I turned back, thirty of his years had passed. Don't ask me what he did during that time; you've heard the speculations. He was supposed to lead a quiet life. Make some furniture. Find a woman and get married (so he could feel desire and love), have children who lived to adulthood (so he could learn pride and joy) and children who died young (so he could learn the five stages of grief). Some rich neighbors (so he could learn envy and greed), some poor neighbors (so he could learn compassion and empathy). And then he would get sick and die (so he could learn fear and patience), a very old man who'd experienced what the planet had to offer.

My brother went off script. Stepped into synagogues and showed off, amassed that group of sycophants. Attracted extra followers with a so-called miracle now and then. Here's your legs back, here's your ears and eyes. Einstein's Luminous Nazarene! But he only wanted to see their tears and gratitude. And maybe he'd feel something back. When that didn't work, when he felt nothing, he ran off to mope. He should have stuck to carpentry.

Creator sent me to fix things. I found him on a hill above Jericho.

Spot up on PROPHET as JESUS. He wears only a loincloth. He drags the lawn chair downstage and squats in it.

TWO-STEP: Salut, mon frère. It's been a while.

JESUS: Hey. Sorry I haven't kept in touch. I been a lot busier than I thought.

TWO-STEP: Have you felt anything yet? (*Aside.*) I knew the answer. Yet so much pleasure in asking.

JESUS: It's hard talking to the womenfolk around here. Lot easier with the men.

TWO-STEP: Perhaps it has to do with your style? Father in Heaven this, Son of Man that? Pretending you're casting out demons when you know it's just their own faulty cells—

JESUS: Your voice is hurting my ears. But don't leave. I got to tell you something. Come close. (*Two-Step leans in; Jesus speaks in a low voice.*) I'm getting outta here sooner than planned.

TWO-STEP (*recoiling*):   Your breath smells terrible. You look malnourished. Perhaps you need some fat and protein?

JESUS: Yes siree! Bring me lamb and fig, bread and wine!

TWO-STEP: If you tell them who you are, they'll throw you a banquet. Make you governor. Maybe even king.

JESUS: Tried it. No one believes me. When I was a kid, mother said I'd have all these . . . gifts. Even she done forgot.

TWO-STEP: So put on a big show. Fly around their heads for a while.

JESUS: I forget how. Nah, that's a lie. It's this body. Only so much it can do. Every second it's like a thousand tons on the spine. Don't leave. Lemme lean my head on your shoulder.

TWO-STEP: You need a woman. Or a man. You need to release. Friction of a membrane, spurt of mucus ejected.

JESUS: Yeah, seems that ain't gonna happen.

TWO-STEP: He took my advice, after the wilderness. Put on the Big Lazarus Show. Wept because someday, when he was old, he was going to have to *go through all of that.* He went off to speak with Creator. The two of them came up with a plan. It goes without saying, they did not consult me.

Murder-suicide. That was their plan. A great last-ditch effort: if he couldn't feel love, perhaps he could feel not-hate for the people pounding nails through his wrists and ankles. An infection, a fall, a fight: anything else would have done the job. But why the grotesque display? With his poor mother watching.

Spot up on JESUS. He is on his knees among garden tools and spilled potatoes. Posture of prayer, looking up, entire body shaking.

TWO-STEP: You do *not* have to go through with this. There are painless ways.

JESUS: You don't think I've tried 'em? Has to be done *to* me.

TWO-STEP: Good Lord, you're really sweating. Let me send someone to clean you up.

JESUS: Oh, brother, I'd appreciate that.

JESUS stands, turns rigid. Flings out arms and falls backward in a crucifixion pose. Blackout. In the darkness we hear whisperings, ragged inhales, screams, panting, weeping, groans.

TWO-STEP (*voice magnified above the rest*): Multitudes weeping, myself chief among them.

Brother, my brother!

You know how the rest of the story goes. Borrowed tomb, slab of rock.

Spot up on JESUS at center stage. He is naked. His head is wrapped in gauze.

JESUS: Shit. It didn't take.

TWO-STEP: You gave it your best shot.

JESUS unspools head wrapping, folds it neatly, sets it on the lawn chair. On his back are purple stains that look like wings.

JESUS (*mimes knocking on stone covering exit from tomb*): Ahem. Ahem. Brother. You mind gettin' the door for me?

TWO-STEP's body contorts, his mouth opening in a silent scream. He falls to his knees and fumbles around the floor, feeling for something as if he is blind. He locates a knife, lifts it—his hand shaking violently— and forces himself to carve a giant X into the air.

JESUS steps through the space TWO-STEP has cut open. He embraces TWO-STEP, kissing him on the mouth. He looks up. Deep inhale, exhale. He is lifted into the rafters.

Lights fade to black.

Six

TWO-STEP alone in the cabin. Despondent. Wringing his proverbial hands.

TWO-STEP: I still check in on my brother every so often. He spends most of his time in the South of France. Last time I saw him, though, he was in Russia, in Sergiyev Posad, leaning against a fountain. All those tourists cramming into churches, straining to see him through the icons and missing the actual body with its ancient scars just out in the courtyard. Ever since his departure, my own story has been one long disappearance from the discourse. If the devil gets mentioned, somebody changes the subject. Evolution, natural selection, human biology: these are to blame for the world's suffering. Evil is faulty cells, healing is science. These days it's satanic to believe in Satan. And all the while, belief in the Big Three is on the uptick: Creator, my brother, and the bird my brother trained to ride on his shoulder. (He was that lonely!) Everyone wants heaven.

Three large blades are left to hang. TWO-STEP begins to nail up the last blades as if it is something he must do under threat of death.

TWO-STEP: But the Adversary remains the gateway to eternity. No God without God's opposite. No heaven without hell. I oppose you to give you the chance to live forever. (*Hangs blade, adjusts.*) True, the myth of Satan is finished. But when the giants dissipate, the windmills stand. Why shouldn't it be so with me? (*Hangs tenth blade. Returns to the last, heaviest blade. Drags it to the wall.*) Who is left to believe then? The Watchman. The only one. A just man expelled to the wilds, the world too wide for his shrunk shank, the burden of belief resting on this last beating heart beneath the crumbling edifice. (*Heaves up the eleventh blade.*) And what rough beast will stand to help him bear the weight? (*Fixes the blade in place.*) Me. I will stand. Satan is dead, long live Two-Step!

Seven

TWO-STEP fiddles with the wires attaching the motor to the smallest Ezekiel blade. The PROPHET is in his recliner, shivering beneath a blanket.

PROPHET: You're still here?

TWO-STEP: As you see.

PROPHET: Wish you'd leave.

TWO-STEP: It is written: Never will I leave you, never will I forsake you.

PROPHET: Don't know why you ever showed up here.

TWO-STEP: Misery acquaints a man with strange bedfellows. And had I not shown up to oppose you, your story would have been a different one. I have lifted the curtain on the ordinary, as the book of Job did for—

PROPHET: Leave that alone. Needs one more blade. Michael. You still see her?

TWO-STEP: Yes.

PROPHET: Now?

TWO-STEP: Yes.

PROPHET: Show me.

TWO-STEP: That's the wrong thing to ask.

PROPHET: Don't care about nothin' else.

TWO-STEP: What about the donkeys and beehives?

PROPHET: It's like Zeke said. Them visions was something I made up in my own head.

TWO-STEP: Wrong, sir, wrong! Under section 37-B of the contract drawn up by Creator, any disavowal of your original visons shall be rendered immediately null and void. (*Pulls out parchment.*) This photostatic copy states that all visions will come to pass. In addition, please reference section 111-A, clearly stating that I was sent to act as your adversary to turn your hidden life into a cosmically significant one, in which you would paint, rescue the girl, and send her to the president on behalf of America. And planet Earth.

PROPHET: What've you done to Michael, you two-stepping liar?

TWO-STEP: It is written: without opposition there is no progress!

PROPHET: Damn you and them words.

TWO-STEP: That's it, my beloved, yes. Fight me.

PROPHET: You ain't the one to fight. You ain't even real.

TWO-STEP (*lifts hands in a posture of supplication, Christlike*):   And who do you say that I am?

PROPHET: You're no one. You're nothing. I dreamed you up. (*Lifts his guitar and strums a chord. Begins to sing, hoarsely.*) I heard, the sound, of a-going in the mul-berry tree . . .

TWO-STEP (*aside*):   How I love his childish treble, the pipes and whistles in his sound.

PROPHET (*stops playing*):   Show me the girl.

TWO-STEP: She is not important. She is a means to an end.

PROPHET: Show me the girl, goddamn you!

The PROPHET hurls the guitar at TWO-STEP, who catches it and embraces it like a lover, then sets it on the floor. Attaches one last wire, lifts the motor.

TWO-STEP: Don't say I didn't warn you.

TWO-STEP throws the switch. The sound of machinery coming to life as the smallest wheel begins to spin, catching the one beside it, which likewise spins. At the same moment, the movie screen unscrolls. Hits the floor. Bang. Blades continue to interlock and spin as the screen enlarges and moves forward. Piece by piece, the cabin furniture is pulled into the wings as the screen moves downstage, growing bigger until the stage has disappeared behind it.

We are now in a movie theater. Light projected onto the screen. Sound of film reel.

PICTURE START 8 . . . 7 . . . 6 . . . 5 . . . 4 . . . 3 . . . 2 . . . (Beep.)

Blackout.

Revelation

One is calling to me from Seir,
"Watchman, what time of the night?
Watchman, what time of the night?"

—Isaiah 21:11

Michael bursts through the Greyhound station door, breathless. The wall clock reads 3:26.

The ticket agent tells her the 3:20 bus has just departed. The next one leaves at 7:10—a different route, the agent says, terminating at Port Authority in New York City. Eleven stops, the ninth in Washington, DC.

The New York City bus costs $50 more than the 3:20 bus. But what can she do? She buys the 7:10 ticket.

It's the sitting still that frightens her. She is overcome with exhaustion and she must not fall asleep. She takes out the magazine and reads, again, about the Grand Canyon, the village deep inside. A knot in her stomach, a small nodule about to open. No part of me, she repeats. Not even human. A woman who makes plans. Her own, no one else's. She feels the money in her pocket—and the pills. Now the bus ticket, too. And in her back-pack enough food and water to get there. She looks at the tile floor with its dirty grout and randomly placed orange and blue squares, sees the backs of the mesh metal benches in front of her, listens to the humming of the vending machine. She is here. The old man sending her. Giving her permission. All of it is enough. She feels a lifting, something heavy flying up and away.

(Now the difficult part.
The girl at the bus station. The old man in the woods.
You fleshsacks will want to look away.
You must bear witness.)

Three hours and forty minutes and no one here besides the ticket attendant and a janitor pushing a mop and bucket between restrooms. She lies on her side and tucks her knees up to her chest, making herself small. Pulls her denim jacket over her head and lets her eyes close.

May 19, 2014. The Prophet wakes and stumbles outside. Heat like a giant hand presses down on the Alabama landscape, flattening crops, trees, houses. He stoops beneath its weight. The darkness no longer chimes with crickets or the beady sound of tree frogs. All of them gone. Fled with the girl.

Midnight is so still the Prophet can hear the train whistle all the way down in St. Elmo.

Moonlight shatters the porch, dirt road, dried-out cornstalks.

He goes back inside, swallows some pills and vomits them up. He can feel the crevices in his cheeks when he rubs the back of his hand across his mouth and wipes the sweat off his face with his bandana. He's just settled into his recliner when a dark shape falls from the ceiling, landing with a thud on the floor beside him. He leans over to see the leg of an eagle, a yellow foot with four black claws, one sharp talon opposite the other three. Sicklelike, deadly. The feathers are brown; the grayish bone is visible above what he might call the thigh.

I know what you are, he says to the severed leg. You're all that's left of this country.

The janitor's name is Beth. Her training has taught her to spot the signs of trafficking. In her eighteen months of work, she has identified six victims at this Greyhound station. The girl with the shorn hair and neck tattoo—a flag, the neck tattoo—checks boxes. Dips her head to avoid making eye contact when Beth approaches to mop beneath her bench. The girl covers her face when she lies down to sleep. At 6:30, other passengers begin to fill the waiting area. The girl jolts awake and boards the bus. Beth steps into the restroom, pulls out her phone, and calls the number posted on the stall doors.

May 20. The Prophet wakes up lonely. His ankles are so swollen a touch to the skin with a dull object would cause them to simply open. He yanks down the curtains with the little roses and stuffs them in a corner, then lies on the mattress. The girl's bed. He longs for her scent but can smell nothing but his own decay. He turns this way and that. Sleep will not come. He imagines it's winter, fields bare, oaks and maples showing their forked architecture again, thin topmost branches like the veins in his ankles and the undersides of his wrists. *God, you are a orderly maker*, he thinks. *Twinning the insides of trees and humans.*

Unbearable heat. With effort, he turns onto his stomach so the sweat at the small of his back and in the napes of his knees can dry. He presses his face into the mattress, which turns transparent.

The movie screen unrolls like a carpet beneath him, on the cabin floor.

The donkey appears, once again on top of the planet. His wings are gone, his body bloated, the sides of his torso round as giant saddlebags. The Prophet drags himself up to his hands and knees, looking down at the donkey. Where in God's name have you been? he says.

As the words leave his mouth the donkey bursts. The explosion is so loud the sound is like silence. Unfurling from the donkey's sides, as if from a piñata, are dangling intestines inscribed in black typeface.

ABORTION

POVERTY

MASS SHOOTINGS

FAMINE

WARS AND RUMORS OF WARS

STARVATION

DROUGHT

TEMPESTS

EARTHQUAKE

EARTHQUAKE

EARTHQUAKE

You ain't the president, the Prophet says. You're the whole damn world stuffed with trouble.

Inside the blown-open torso the heart is stuttering, the lungs and stomach and kidneys all injured beyond repair. Blood streams onto the planet beneath the failing body, melting the polar ice. Greenland and Iceland, Canada and Alaska, Russia and Scandinavia—countries and continents dissolving beneath the blood pumping unevenly from the wretched dying heart.

Someone's got to put you down! the Prophet cries.

The donkey looking at him. The great hovering tears.

With effort the Prophet stands. He takes the double-barrel from its pegs and loads two shells. He points the gun straight down into the mattress until he feels the barrel against the floor. He leans against the butt end with his good shoulder.

Shot, shot.

The movie screen rolls up.

Too late!

World's about to burst! he cries.

When it explodes, the Prophet knows he'll be gone.

And who will be the one to put the donkey down?

Michael keeps her face pressed to the window, watching the twilit hills of East Tennessee scroll past, scenes she has only dreamed of. Latticed white houses tucked into dark crevices like bits of lace. Sheep and horses, stands of trees surrounding red-roofed barns. After dark, the glowing webs of small cities. The bus stops in Charlotte, Salisbury, Winston-Salem, Greensboro. Bodies get on and off. The girl stops paying attention. She takes another pill. *Get on the right bus and all you got to do is stay on.*

In Durham, a woman wearing joggers and a Georgetown sweatshirt boards. She carries a backpack, has her hair pulled up in a high ponytail, wears a fashionable pair of clear-rimmed glasses, and black Chuck Taylors, low-tops. This not-quite-young woman walks down the aisle snapping her gum, scanning faces. She locates the shorn hair and the denim jacket, the backpack beneath the seat. She tosses her own backpack into the overhead across. And while the girl sleeps in the swaying hammock of the cushioned bus seat—the kind of extinguished, annihilating sleep that comes only to the very young or the very exhausted—she texts her colleague in Richmond: *Victim ID'd. ETA 12:40 am.*

Shot, shot.

The Prophet is full of energy: the pain in his back and side gone, a magnificent power restored to his limbs. When he smells the smoke and sees Two-Step in his corner, the Prophet nearly chokes with joy.

Welcome home, friend! he says.

The devil has aged. His jowls are cobwebbed with lines, his jeans loose around his thighs. The silver-toed boots tap-tap-tapping the wood floor.

How'd you like to take a walk with me? the Prophet says.

Two-Step straightens his bolo and puts on his cowboy hat. Together, they walk down to St. Elmo. Not a single car passes. The parks are empty. Swing seats dangle motionless from their chains. They go from house to house, doors left ajar or hanging loose from hinges. They wander from room to room: dinners laid out on tables, Christmas trees twinkling with lights, presents wrapped and stacked beneath.

Where are the children this been prepared for? the Prophet says.

Two-Step is silent beside him.

We're vanishing a nation in silence, the Prophet says.

The Prophet and Two-Step return to the cabin. The air hangs chill and wet over the field, blue-gray fog caught in leafless branches like smoke. How did they get back here so fast? When did it become winter? They climb the porch steps. The Prophet holds the door open, but Two-Step removes his hat and makes a low bow. Don't leave me, the Prophet says—but already the black smoke is curling around the dead tomato plants, rising between the porch beams, dissolving into the gray wetness of sky.

The Prophet stumbles inside.

Michael, he cries out. Zeke!

Sometimes he cries out his own name, the long-ago name no one remembers. *Winston!* His voice makes no sound the living can hear.

An hour outside of Richmond, the woman in the Georgetown sweatshirt wakes the girl to ask if she has a tampon. Sorry to bug you, it wasn't supposed to come this early but anyhow what a relief, I mean me and my boyfriend use protection but sometimes we sort of, like, slip? And sometimes it's like, you know. Other guys besides him, hookups at parties and shit. Means nothing. Even if he knew he wouldn't care. You go to UVA?

And the girl, in her buoyed condition, knowing she's on the right bus, almost to step eight, *planned*—how she loves the sound of it, *women who make plans*, and maybe this Georgetown student would know where it is, even give her a ride—in this condition she will let her guard down.

She will tell the Georgetown student everything. King, Jessamine. The old man in the woods, his visions and paintings. How he rescued her and helped her get clean, but when she realized she might be pregnant she had to drive herself to steal a test. Had to be sure, right? A long way to go to a state where *no waiting no parents no judge has to excuse*. Then him giving her the money for Washington, saying it was her job.

Like it was God saying it's okay, Michael says.

She tells the student about the Grand Canyon, Jackson. Shows her Zeke's phone. Her sentences rush one into the other. The sheer relief of telling makes her heart beat so fast she has to gulp air between words.

He's harmless, Zeke says. Crazy, but harmless. He wouldn't have done anything to hurt her.

Nashville, May 21. In Zeke's living room, the detectives—alerted by social services, who took possession of the girl's phone in Richmond—take notes. Zeke describes the mailbox with the the bear holding a honeycomb and gives them the name of the last church before the turnoff.

The detectives explain that he may have to testify.

I'll drive up with y'all, Zeke says. I've got some questions for him myself.

I knew he'd end up doing something like this, Zeke's wife says after the detectives have left.

Sullivan sits in the darkened hallways upstairs. She is supposed to be asleep, but these men have been talking about the grandfather she's never met, the one who used to send her candy and dollar bills. She still writes to him. She tells him about riding horses after school, and her teacher who wears fuzzy slippers sometimes, just for fun, and about her best friend named Maddy. *When will you come to visit?* she writes. Inside each envelope she puts a little present: a colored leaf, a pressed flower, a drawing of her horse. She doesn't know his address but writes on the envelopes: *To Grampa*. She gives the envelopes to her father to mail.

In Chattanooga, a team is dispatched. Four cop cars, a fire truck, an ambulance. At dusk their lights snake up Ochs Highway. They won't turn on the sirens until their headlights hit the WATCHMAN sign outlined in reflective tape.

At the home for women in Knoxville, Michael is given a private room. A stuffed lion wearing real sunglasses waits on the bed, a handwritten note of welcome propped between its legs. Above the headboard is a monthly tear-off calendar with ladybugs painted around its perimeter: it is here she is supposed to mark down her prenatal vitamins, her doctor visits, her appointments with the trauma counselor, the adoption agency.

Everyone here is kind. You have an opportunity, they tell her. A counselor shows Michael pictures of translucent fetuses sucking their thumbs. Your baby is the size of a mushroom cap, she says, with a beating heart like a seed tucked up inside its folds. A nurse squeezes cold gel onto Michael's stomach and slides a device shaped like an electric razor over her skin, uncovering a ghostly swish. *Wowowowowowow.* The sound of the ceiling fan above her bed at the foster home in Macon.

There is a computer lab, a salon, and a gym, where once a week she will take a prenatal yoga class. There are classrooms where she will have geography and history and art lessons. The hallways are painted with roses taller than she is. Butterflies the size of German shepherds.

Most of the women here are older. Some beaten up by their husbands. Some coming off street drugs: meth and heroin. Many are homeless. *I am nothing like them*, she thinks. It will be years before she understands.

Mandarin orange, lime, beefsteak tomato.

In her shorts and T-shirt, you'd never know. She knows. The bulge of her areolas, red ripples in the skin along her sides. In the shower she refuses to look down at herself.

Tremorings inside her, at night, like whatever is in there has caught a chill.

How selfless she is, everyone keeps saying. How brave. You're giving life to so many people, they say, not just to the baby.

Brave, she tells herself. *Selfless*. She cannot believe that what is growing inside of her will ever make anyone happy.

She is wrong. The baby will bring so much happiness to so many people, the weight of it will knock the solar system off course.

(And this is the complication for you fleshsacks, isn't it? You cannot stand for the horrific and the beautiful to touch, cannot fathom a system in which one person benefits from the suffering of another. But so it is. So Creator has ordained. What a pathetic state he's left you in.)

Six weeks early, in the middle of the night—the last day of November—the first contraction hits. Michael jolts upright in bed, something hot and metallic clamped around her waist. When the pain subsides, she rolls off the mattress and crawls to the toilet, lying in darkness on the tile, knees curled to her chest. When the next contraction barrels into her back, she cries out until the woman in the room beside her comes in and flicks on the light. Hang on, I'll get someone, she says, running out again. Wait, Michael says. Wait. But something like cloud shadow passes through her, from her scalp to her feet, a wave unfurling outward through her fingertips. She gets up on her hands and knees to let what she believes is urine stream down her legs. The nurse arrives with a wheelchair and checks between her legs. I want the drugs, Michael says. Don't push, the nurse says. The birthing rooms are one building over, three floors up. Michael clings to the arms of the wheelchair, the sound of moaning—she knows it's her own—following just behind. The elevator opens, two nurses are waiting, they get her onto a bed and remove the lower half of the mattress, helping her place her feet in metal holds. *Not yet not yet*—but there's nothing she can do, the pain is forcing her down into the bed, inside herself, she cannot float up like before, she must go into the darkness of the squeezing burning, all of her concentrated into the hot searing tearing between her thighs. A thick wet slipping and it's over. The thing is out. She does not want to see it, does not want to know the sex, and when it's taken out of the room she feels nothing but relief. A nurse massages her stomach while another inserts an IV. You did good, sweetie, she says, stroking her forehead. You can sleep now. Her legs are quivering. She can't make them stop. An orderly with dangling cherry-shaped earrings pulls socks on her feet: beige, with rubbery bottoms that cling to the metal stirrups. *Such ugly socks*, Michael thinks, before losing consciousness.

While Michael sleeps, the doctor arrives, disheveled, wearing sweats. He pulls on a gown and gloves and magnifying goggles. Rolls a stool between the legs to deliver the placenta while a nurse adjusts the goose-necked lamp to illuminate the damage.

There have been some beautiful stories. They are the stories told at fundraising dinners. He tries to remember just one of those stories now. On the record, he supports the mission. Off the record, he has sent girls this age to doctor friends who are willing to look the other way. Off the record, he believes what this girl has just endured is a nightmare. He lifts his needle driver and tissue forceps and begins to stitch her up.

Against all odds, the baby is a perfect creature. Six pounds two ounces, bald and pink. Two immediate tens on the Apgar scale. The washed body sparkles with fuzz, the tiny legs kick and kick. A nurse diapers and swaddles, then deftly pulls a pink-striped beanie cap over the glowing ears.

When she sees her adopted daughter for the first time, the young mother thinks of the jeweled interior of some ruby-red fruit. The father, a podiatrist, frees the kicking legs and runs his finger up and down the baby's sole. The new parents want to thank the teenager who gave her up, but the arrangement stipulates no contact. The mother writes an elaborate letter anyhow. She tells the birth mother how their own son died right after he was born. A late-forming hemangioma—strawberry birthmark, harmless when formed on the body's exterior—had taken root on the trachea sometime during the last trimester. It grew at an exponential rate, filling the throat so that when the time came, the lungs could not expand. Twelve minutes from time of birth to time of death.

It's my fault he died, she writes to the birth mother. *My husband wanted an obstetrician, but I insisted on doing everything without medical intervention. Home birth, doula, bathtub.* No sonograms the last trimester. *Had we done it his way there would have been a chance.* She tells the birth mother how she paced the house for days, then weeks, thinking only of her dead son and how his life was an image of every life. *We're born, we struggle to breathe, we give up.* How the thought of his twelve minutes led her, twice, to attempt to join him, wherever he was. Not enough pills—or enough of the right kind of pills.

I believe God kept me alive for this, she writes. *For your baby. Ours.*

I will think of you every day for the rest of my life, she writes.

The letter, of course, is never sent.

The week before Christmas, Michael is placed with a family in Knoxville. Three children, all of them younger. In January she is supposed to join the eighth grade with the oldest of the children. But she is fifteen now. Too old for eighth grade.

Grand Canyon, she thinks.

Jackson.

Oh, my beauty, my love, Kingston says when she calls one of the two numbers she has memorized.

One month after Michael's arrival, the foster mother finds her bed made, her clothing gone, not even a note on the pillow.

The baby's name is Charlotte. Charlie for short. The young mother gets up in the night and holds the girl to her chest just to feel the steady, rapid breath. The house glitters with Christmas lights. On the tree hangs a giraffe with a pacifier around its neck: CHARLIE'S FIRST CHRISTMAS, 2014. A week after they bring her home, the young father, in a sudden burst of joy, buys a slot car track and puts it together at the foot of the crib. The slick electric whizz seems to calm her. When his daughter begins to crawl he will break it down and put it away until she is past the age of choking, and then he will bring it out again, and the two of them will race slot cars together, the tracks becoming more and more elaborate, until she leaves for college.

She will stand at eight months, walk at ten. At a year old she will be running. In elementary school she will run faster than anyone in any of her PE classes; as a freshman in high school she will win the state track championship in the 400. The mother will be overwhelmed each time she watches her daughter run. Watches her do anything. It's as if she's being lifted upward, painfully, by a string threaded in through her navel and out through her heart. Tugging and tugging her chest to the sky. She tells herself that if the birth mother could see her daughter as she is now, she would do everything the same all over again.

This love is not uncomplicated. When Charlie is fourteen, she asks to meet her own mother. My *real* mother, she says, not you, not you! But her parents can't help her. We're sorry, they say. We don't know who, where, we don't know anything about her.

Charlie journals into the night. Only once does her mother read the entries, devastated and furious that this girl—this daughter—to whom they've given everything could write such hateful things. She allows herself to wonder from time to time if the best thing, after all, would have been for Charlie to stay with her birth mother, no matter how young. Never once does she let herself consider the alternative, if the birth mother had made a different choice.

Let us consider it.

Begin with the Honorable James D. Rhodes, chief judge of the Eastern District of Tennessee, sixty-four years old. When the new girl appears at the bar in the Texas Lounge, the judge—Panda-man—asks her what happened to the last girl.

Angel who? the new girl says.

The one before you, the judge says. The one in the blond wig.

The girl's eyes narrow. Would you like me to call my manager? she asks.

That won't be necessary, Judge Rhodes says.

What's your name, darling, he says, placing a hand on her stockinged thigh.

The following day he considers turning himself in. But too many people would be hurt. His family and career destroyed. And this new girl isn't as young as the last; nor does she remind him of a daughter or a granddaughter. The next time he logs in to his Backpage account, he requests a new engagement point. Transfers his meetings to a restaurant on Broad Street across from the Sheraton.

From time to time, he thinks about the last girl, the panda bear purse stuffed with cash, the hiding place inside the life jacket. He considers going back for it, maybe leaving a note for the girl so she can get help. But he tells himself she's likely made off with it. That she is, at this very moment, making a better life for herself. He tells himself this story so often, he comes to believe it has happened.

Continues on as before.

And so the purse is fat with cash when Michael arrives. She grabs it and runs. No need to hitchhike. She hails a cab on the busy road beside the park and makes it to the Greyhound station in time. When the janitor comes on shift, Michael has been on the road for an hour.

And there are actual college students on the bus. One of them has just finished her freshman year at Washington and Lee, a double major in anthropology and history. Her name is Ellie and she's from DC, the oldest of three siblings whose parents taught their children that, yes, there is some black and white, but mostly there is gray, gray, gray. Who told them to be kind to strangers, for you may be entertaining angels unaware.

It is to Ellie that Michael will divulge her story. Sentences rushing one into the next, gulping air. Ellie does a quick search on her phone.

The clinic is twelve minutes from the station, she says, like *literally* on the way to my house. I'm sure my parents will give you a ride.

I have cab money, Michael says.

Oh, take the Metro, it's way cheaper, Ellie says.

She gives Michael her phone number.

Let me know how it goes, Ellie says. If, like, you need a place to stay or whatever.

At the clinic, she is given another test to confirm. She watches a film that tells her what to expect. Afterward, a nurse with blue-framed glasses asks her a series of questions. She speaks with a British accent, calling her *love*. She explains the procedure again and, when she is finished explaining, gives Michael the papers to sign. No signature required but her own. She uses a made-up name. Her choice to undo what she did not choose.

They give her antibiotics. Pain pills, a sting to numb.

Still, the undoing is painful. A nurse holds her hand.

She's in the recovery area when a girl comes in with her mother. The girl is sobbing. Michael cannot believe how young she looks—younger even than she is herself. She moans and cries out while a nurse helps her get onto the bed.

Cramping is normal, the nurse says, but we're getting you something for the pain.

Thank you, the mother says.

When the nurse is gone, the mother and daughter begin to speak in a language Michael doesn't recognize.

Ça fait vraiment mal, the girl says, personne ne m'a dit que ce serait si douleureux!

T'inquiète pas, the mother says. Ce sera bientôt fini.

Ça fait mal—

Calme-toi ma puce, the mother says.

The woman looks at Michael.

Your mother, she is with you? she asks.

I don't have a mother, Michael says.

The woman walks over and places her hand on the blanket covering Michael's torso.

Aujourd'hui c'est moi ta mère, she says. *Today, I am your mother.*

(So much kindness among you fleshsacks, is what I'm saying. You forget this. You polarize, call something evil and forget the goodness the evil engenders. You call something good and forget the evil the good depends on. But the kindness! If you counterbalanced all the kindness with the evils you keep putting before your eyes—your newspapers and TVs, apps and websites—you would not recognize your own planet.)

Often Michael thinks of the old man in the cabin. The Watchman. She never knew his real name.

Three weeks after the procedure, when she's living with a host family in Georgetown, she remembers the old phone and finds the right kind of charger. When the screen blazes up there is, of course, no service. But the Wi-Fi works. A single contact in the address book—the name she was hoping to see. She texts:

Is this Zeke
Who is this?
Your dad took care of me
You the girl he kidnapped???
Rescued

She deletes and retypes:

RESCUED!
What's your name?

[. . .]

Can I call you
No service
Do you have another number
No
Okay listen, the police found him dead.

[. . .]

Shotgun. He wouldn't have lasted long the way he
    was anyhow.
I'm sorry he was nice to me nicer than anyone
If you tell me who you are I can
Please do not get rid of his paintings!

She turns off the phone, leaves the house and walks
to Waterfront Park, and—from an overlook on the
promenade—drops it into the Potomac.

Michael's ACT scores are only just above average, but
because of her personal essay she wins a scholarship to
Georgetown. She majors in art history, and when everything shuts down, she thinks, fleetingly, of the pig with
the toilet paper in its mouth, the lizard with light bulb eyes
and the words *I TOLD YOU SO* scrolling down its tongue.
She remembers the title: *Plague in Dogwood Season.*

After graduating she moves to New York and lives
with four roommates in Bushwick, working in a Lower
East Side gallery until she gets a higher-paying job at a
blue chip in Chelsea. She has the gallery look, they tell
her. Tall and waiflike, with a beguiling kind of sadness
that comes off as nonchalance. Above all, her boss says,
artists and collectors alike are drawn to indifference.

The gallery pays for her to get an M.A. in art history in exchange for a commitment to work for two
years after she finishes. She's named research associate.

A year later, when the Whitney posts an opening for a curatorial assistant, she applies for and gets the job. One day in a planning meeting, the head curator of postwar American art mentions a retrospective on outsider art planned for 2028. After the meeting, Michael returns to her desk and googles: Johnny Cash performers Nashville.

Zeke is easy, easy to find.

She sends an email.

Remember me?

She mentions the name of the museum and a possible sum for the paintings. Zeke sends a link to Dropbox filled with images.

She takes the images to the head curator.

My God, he says, scrolling. Where did you *find* this guy?

Friend of a friend, she lies. He's dead, though.

All the better, the curator says.

A team from the museum is dispatched to Atlanta. Michael, of course, goes with them. They rent a van and drive up Lookout Mountain, following the route Michael remembers.

Turn at the bear-and-honeycomb mailbox, she says. Follow the dirt road into the woods.

The cabin is filled with dust, cobwebs, rotting debris. Kudzu and other weeds grow thick between the split planks. Broken windows, doors hanging from hinges. The rose curtains are gone, the mattress and chair are gone, the cupboards and drawers emptied. Otherwise the cabin is as she remembers: paintings covering the walls and ceiling, tree of life in the center. Ezekiel wheels leaning against a wall, furred with rust.

An assistant swipes one of the sawblades with a rag, revealing the eyeball.

Holy *shit*, she says. This place is a fucking gold mine.

Plank by plank, the cabin is dismantled, packed into shipping crates, and sent to New York, where it is reinstalled in the factory-sized addition at the Whitney, constructed for the retrospective. Michael herself oversees the installation. She frames the little booklet of visions the old man drew for her, which she's kept for all these years as a reminder of his kindness, though she can't remember what any of the drawings mean, or why he felt they were so important. She draws a schematic of the Ezekiel wheels and orders the smallest blade, the twelfth, from Home Depot: *Diablo Steel Demon*, 7¼-inch. An artist is commissioned to cover it in gold leaf and paint the eyeball.

The machine is mounted, twelve wheels left spinning, day and night.

Before the opening, above the front door, Michael hangs the announcement board—his beautiful idea!—the board she wrote and painted herself, fourteen years earlier.

(But you fleshsacks aren't fooled. You know how this works.

Let us—finally—return to the truth.)

The birth, adoption, temporary placement in Knoxville. The call to King, who meets Michael at a Krispy Kreme off I-24.

Where's Jackson? she asks.

King's open hand. The pills and peaceful feeling. She doesn't mention the name again.

King confiscates what little money she has left; the booklet of visions is lost.

In Chattanooga, the *Delta Queen* closes. Windows are boarded up, gangways removed. In early 2015, the boat will be towed down into the Mississippi Delta, with plans for a refit so it can resume operations as a tour boat. This will never happen, and the *Delta Queen* will end up permanently docked in Houma, Louisiana.

Michael works in and around Atlanta and Macon. Two years, three, until there's a tip-off. An undercover sex worker whose john is a high school soccer coach. King is arrested, prosecuted, and—after entering a guilty plea—is sentenced by a U.S. district judge to twenty-seven years and six months in federal prison, to be followed by ten years supervised release.

Restitution payments of $7,500 are made to each victim.

Counselors, clinical social workers, halfway houses.

When Michael turns eighteen, she decides to hitch-hike west. She works at diners in Birmingham, Meridian, Midland, Las Cruces. Eventually she makes it all the way to Tucson, where she gets a job waiting tables at Trail Dust Town. At night crooners come through with their guitars and banjos and sing about lost loves and purple skies. Sometimes she's asked to fill in at the shoot-'em-up show. She plays the part of a barmaid, wears long skirts and a high-necked blouse; on cue she pushes open the saloon doors and steps onto the porch, holding a tray of drinks. When the outlaw shoots the sheriff, she drops the tray and faints dramatically.

None of it pays enough to live on.

And she's good at other things.

It is not a life without dignity.

(This is a story we all know. Don't you dare call it a crime.)

Epilogue

May 21, 2014. The Prophet stands in the doorway of his cabin, breathing deeply. He's never felt this strong, never in his whole life. *Better to be alive thisaway*, he thinks. *Awake and ready to welcome the girl back.*

The body he left on the mattress is starting to rot. He feels a kind of tenderness toward the cement-colored face and wasted limbs. Well done, good and faithful, he tells it. He wishes the ears could hear.

He lifts his guitar and sits in his rocker. Michael's chair beside him, bearing her name.

He sees the headlights first. Then the trees light up red and blue and sirens begin to ring. At last, at last! They've found her. They're bringing Michael home.

The Prophet strums a few chords and tunes the strings. He'll be ready, should these people need to hear his song.

Acknowledgments

Anna Stein, thank you for believing in this book from the beginning, and for reminding me, over and over, to trust my own voice and vision. Elisabeth Schmitz, the patience and care you take with my words is astonishing. I'll never get over how lucky I am to get to work with you. Let's always edit at your dining room table? Morgan Entrekin, Judy Hottensen, Deb Seager, John Mark Boling, Laura Schmitt, Gretchen Mergenthaler, Mike Richards, Natalie Church, Rachael Richardson, JT Green, and the rest of my Grove family: thank you, as ever, for championing my work. Thanks to Katie Raissian for reading on your way out, and to Paula Cooper Hughes for your thoughtful and nuanced copy-edits. Thank you to Sophie Lambert, Claire Nozieres, and Zoe Willis for representing my work in foreign territories. MacDowell and Yaddo, thank you for giving me time and space and *literal* magic: studio visits from benignant black bears, rainbows above gravestones, the right book on the right shelf at the very moment I needed it. I'm especially grateful to the Corporation of Yaddo for awarding me the 2023 Michael and Nina Sundell Residency.

Endless gratitude to Tom Bissell, David Gates, Garth Greenwell, Lauren Groff, Samantha Harvey, Elliott Holt, Leslie Jamison, and John McElwee. Thank you to Stephen Prothero at Boston University for reading the manuscript with an eye toward theological accuracy, and to Giles Waller and Sophie Lunn-Rockliffe at Cambridge University for help with the devil. Thanks to Louis Myers for sharing your welding knowledge; April and Stephen Alvarez for help with archival issues of *National Geographic* and paleolithic artwork; Claire Vassort, Geoffrey Cohen, and Ludovic Lusseau for your help with French translation; and Jason Reed at Aladdin for all those copies over the years. Henri Lowe, thank you for fact-checking the manuscript—you went above and beyond the call of duty, and did so with an excitement that was contagious.

Tory Hood and Brittney Giannunzio, formerly with Second Life Chattanooga, thank you for sharing your expertise and experiences. Thank you to Jason and Shelly Lewis for spearheading the meeting, and for the tough conversations about sex trafficking criminals in our city and region. Thank you to Kristin Beckum at Thistle Farms, Nashville, for sharing your personal journey.

Thank you to my children and children-in-law, McKenna, Ryan, Keaton, Jess, Hallie-Blair, and Hudson.

You've listened to me talk about this book over the years to the point of exasperation. Not one of you acted exasperated. Heroic. Special thanks to my daughter Hallie-Blair and my brother Johnny Utz for being thoughtful early readers. And to my beloved Scott: you're the reason I kept going on this one. You're the Reason.

Finally, to my good friend Ralph: I'm so glad I pulled over for pumpkins fifteen years ago. Thank you for welcoming me into your home whenever I show up, and for sharing your paintings and visions and world with me. You are a true artist.